Jesse fought to

But the other vehicle locked onto their truck.

The front tires hit grass, bouncing and shaking the entire cab like it might fall apart—or flip—any minute.

In seconds it was over. The truck rolled to a stop.

Then a car door slammed shut right behind them. Sadie's gaze flew to Jesse's, her eyes wide. The two men from the ranch stalked toward the truck, each carrying a gun.

Jesse jerked back around, his foot slamming the gas at the same moment. The engine roared to life and the tires spun as the truck strained to separate from the SUV locked onto its bumper. Metal creaked. If they could just break free...

Outside, one of the men yelled something and a gunshot split the air, followed by secondary sharp bangs. The truck listed forward, its tires instantly deflating. Another shot shattered the already damaged rear window, showering glass onto Jesse and across Sadie's back as she hunched over.

They were trapped.

Kellie VanHorn is an award-winning author of inspirational romance and romantic suspense. She has college degrees in biology and nautical archaeology, but her sense of adventure is most satisfied by a great story. When not writing, Kellie can be found homeschooling her four children, camping, baking and gardening. She lives with her family in western Michigan.

Books by Kellie VanHorn

Love Inspired Suspense

Fatal Flashback
Buried Evidence
Hunted in the Wilderness
Dangerous Desert Abduction
Treacherous Escape
Wyoming Ranch Sabotage

Visit the Author Profile page at LoveInspired.com.

WYOMING RANCH SABOTAGE

KELLIE VANHORN

LOVE INSPIRED SUSPENSE
INSPIRATIONAL ROMANCE

LOVE INSPIRED® SUSPENSE
INSPIRATIONAL ROMANCE

ISBN-13: 978-1-335-98046-5

Wyoming Ranch Sabotage

Copyright © 2025 by Kellie VanHorn

Love Inspired
22 Adelaide St. West, 41st Floor
Toronto, Ontario M5H 4E3, Canada
www.LoveInspired.com

Printed in Lithuania

Recycling programs
for this product may
not exist in your area.

MIX
Paper | Supporting
responsible forestry
FSC® C021394

It is of the Lord's mercies that we are not consumed,
because his compassions fail not. They are
new every morning: great is thy faithfulness.
—*Lamentations* 3:22–23

In memory of Kippy, Sasha, Madison
and all the other loyal, furry companions
we've loved and said goodbye to far too soon.

Acknowledgments

Thank you so much to the wonderful team
who makes these books possible:
my editor, Katie Gowrie; my agent, Ali Herring; and
my critique partner extraordinaire, Kerry Johnson.
Also, my endless thanks to my husband and kids
for your support, and especially to my son Nate
for sharing your expertise about the Tetons and
helping me brainstorm the best ways to get Jesse
and Sadie into trouble on the trails. Love you all!

ONE

The brass table clock ticked softly as Sadie Madsen rubbed bleary eyes with her ink-stained fingers. Nearly midnight. She *should* be sound asleep, not staring at this ledger that was never going to balance in her favor. Yet again, her frayed nerves and crumbling financial state had kept her up well beyond a reasonable bedtime.

Kip, her rough collie, unfurled his long pink tongue in a yawn before resettling on the area rug in a pile of golden brown and white fur. In the distance, a horse whinnied. Butterscotch?

"Sorry, boy," she said to the dog. "I'll go to bed soon. Promise." *Just as soon as I figure out how to get the ranch back on track.*

Double M Ranch—named after her grandfather, Morris Madsen—had taken one hit after another since her parents' deaths in a car accident four years ago. Cattle vanishing through broken fencing. The mysterious waterborne illness that killed off a quarter of the herd before they identified it. Rising hay prices. Rising everything prices. It was nearly enough to make her consider one of the many offers she'd received from potential buyers.

When she'd found the brake line severed on one of her

ATVs last month, she'd *almost* gone to the police. What if one of those would-be buyers was trying to force the issue? After all, how could one ranch have this many "accidents"? Her shoulder still ached occasionally from the hay bale that had fallen on her six weeks ago.

But what would the authorities be able to do without evidence of foul play? A rock could've cut the line. The hay bale might've been stacked improperly, even though her instincts told her someone had sneaked inside and shifted it. But in the end, despite the uneasiness constantly gnawing at her, she'd decided to keep it to herself until she had some kind of proof.

Her gaze skidded across the desk, landing on the letter from the geologist's office, half-buried in papers and torn envelopes. A single, tangible piece of hope and regret.

What had she been thinking, getting the land evaluated? Sure, they'd told her exactly what she'd hoped to hear: *Most likely you've got oil here, Ms. Madsen. You could be a very wealthy woman.* But what was she going to do about it? She couldn't exactly afford to set up a drilling operation, and an ugly rig next to her house wasn't going to attract guests to her property the way she wanted.

Situated in Jackson Hole, Wyoming, Double M had a gorgeous view of the Tetons, access to a tributary feeding into the Snake River, and thousands of acres of prime land. Perfect for opening the ranch to guests *if* she could find the cash to renovate. It had been her secret dream ever since college when she'd spent a weekend with her roommate's family at their guest ranch in the Bighorn Mountains. The simple luxury, the welcoming environment, the way visitors left inspired and refreshed—she'd caught that vision for the Double M.

Convincing her parents to get on board had been another matter. They'd always viewed it as "someday" project. But at this rate, just keeping the place in operation was in question. Selling only the mineral rights was an option, but she hated the idea of splitting the family estate after all these generations.

A second horse whinnied, startling her out of her thoughts and setting her on edge. Clyde this time, but something had been off about the sound. Higher pitched, as if the horse were afraid.

Kip jerked upright, his head alert and eyes bright. Her exhaustion vanished as adrenaline pulsed through her system. Did they smell a wolf outside the barn? Hear a coyote?

Or was someone on her land?

The collie popped up onto all fours, sniffing the air. A low growl rattled his throat, sending a chill skating up Sadie's arms.

She shoved her chair back from the desk and dashed to the gun storage locker to pull out a rifle, then sprinted for the front door with Kip at her heels. It would be a whole lot easier just to check the video feed for her security cameras, but the whole system had gone down last year, and she hadn't scraped together the money to replace it yet.

Zeke Nelson, the ranch foreman, was away on a long weekend to visit his daughter and new grandson, so she'd have to handle this situation on her own. He and his wife, Lottie, lived in the old bunkhouse behind the main house, while the rest of the hands—the ones she could still afford to pay—commuted to the ranch each day.

Her throat tightened as she reached the front door. Orange glowed through the glass panes. The horse barn stood roughly eighty yards from the house, on the other side of the gravel turnaround and an exercise paddock. And it was on fire.

A choking sense of panic nearly strangled her. Not the horses! *Please, Lord, protect them. Save the brand-new barn.* She'd spent *years* scrimping to pull enough out of the operating budget to make this building happen.

Sadie's feet felt rooted to the spot as she stared at the dancing flames in horror. By the time the fire department got all the way out here, it would be too late.

A lone thought spurred her into action. *Save the horses.*

She stuffed the rifle into an umbrella rack and flung the door open. A waft of acrid smoke drifted on the chilly early June breeze, and Kip whined. Tongues of fire crackled and sparked against a backdrop of black sky and winking stars. There was no time to waste unless she wanted to lose her best horses, too.

"Kip, stay," she commanded, then closed the door before he could follow her out of the house. The last thing she needed was to worry about him getting injured or caught underfoot. She sprinted across the gravel drive, rocks biting into her bare feet. Then cool, dewy grass hit her soles for a few strides before she vaulted over the paddock fence and across the exercise yard.

Her hands slammed into the heavy sliding barn doors, and she yanked one open. A burst of heat and smoke hit her in the face. She coughed, pulling her shirt up over her mouth.

Inside, the horses stamped and pawed in their stalls, their terrified whinnies rising like the smoke.

"I'm here. I'll get you out," she called, running from one stall to the next, opening the doors.

Hooves thundered across the floor as each one bolted for the wide-open barn entrance.

In the far corner, where the fire appeared to have started, flames rippled blue and white and yellow along the surface of the crossbeams. One of them creaked ominously.

Heat scorched her face as she worked her way deeper into the barn. Smoke streamed upward over her head, and the biting smell burned her nostrils and made her eyes water. At least she could still breathe, thanks to the high vaulted roof overhead. Now there were only a few animals left near the end of the barn closest to the fire.

As Sadie approached the big black stallion Orion—her high-strung stud—he reared up on his hind legs. The whites of his eyes reflected the glowing amber flames.

"Whoa, boy!" she called over the crackling. When she pulled the stall door open, the stallion burst out. Timbers groaned nearby, and a loud *thunk* sounded in the other direction. Had Orion made it outside?

No time to look now. There were still two horses left— her oldest animals, quarter horses Bonnie and Clyde. The docile mare had been her mother's favorite, and Sadie had roped her first calf on Clyde's steady back.

She released Bonnie, then turned for the next stall. But as she reached for the latch, a section of the flaming roof gave way, collapsing onto the floor nearby. Sizzling bits of debris flew through the air, pelting her arms as she threw them over her face.

Clyde's high-pitched whinny tore through the barn and Sadie's soul.

An answering whinny came from the end near the barn door—why hadn't her mother's mare left? Was Bonnie waiting for the gelding?

"Come on, boy, we've got to go!" She tugged open Clyde's door and whipped out of the way as he cantered for the other end of the barn.

The smoke was building now as the fire spread, making it hard to see, and she ducked low to keep her face out of it. Her eyes burned, sending tears streaming down her cheeks.

More frenzied whinnies from the far end. Were the horses too panicked to find the way out? She ran after them, dodging open stall doors until she neared the entrance. They stamped their hooves in terror, blocking her view of the doors.

"Whoa!" she called, keeping her voice calm despite her racing heart. "Bonnie. Clyde. Let me get you out. The door's open."

But when she finally ducked and darted her way between them, she found that somehow the sliding door had fallen shut. The cool night, with its twinkling stars and the soft glow of the ranch house, was hidden behind solid wood. How on earth? Had one of the other horses somehow kicked it closed? Or—

Had someone shut her inside? A vise gripped her ribs. Her own death wasn't the kind of proof she wanted to provide the police.

"Stay back, Bonnie. Clyde, watch out. Come on, you two, let me get it open," she ordered as she fumbled for the handle. She leaned back, tugging on the heavy door with her full weight when it didn't slide open easily on the first attempt. Zeke kept those rails so well-oiled they were smooth as an ice rink. It shouldn't take this much force.

Had the heat warped the rails? But that didn't make sense—the fire was at the opposite end of the barn, and the heat was only now working its way across the enclosed space. She tried the other door. It wouldn't open, either.

Panic flared beneath her ribs, momentarily clouding any sense of reason. As if they could sense her fear, the two horses reared again, and she pulled backward against the nearest stall to avoid getting kicked.

Calm down, she told herself, then prayed, *Lord, please help us get out.*

She drew in a deep breath to slow her racing heart, but the smoke burned her throat and made her cough. When she'd recovered, she tried the doors again. Neither budged. As if they'd been locked from the outside.

They were trapped.

Swallowing down her panic, she spun on her heel. The stalls had Dutch doors that opened into exercise paddocks on both sides. If she could just get to the nearest one, they could all get out.

She slid past the hysterical horses and into the first stall, her hip bumping the grain bin on its rack. After crossing the twelve-by-twelve space, she found the outside latch on the door and threw it open. Then she flung open the Dutch door and sucked in a quick breath of fresh air.

Clyde's whickering was the only warning that the horses had followed her into the stall. Eleven hundred pounds of horseflesh barreled past her, slamming her sideways. Sadie's head smacked into the metal rack holding the grain bin on the wall, and tiny silver stars dotted her vision seconds before everything went black.

Jesse Taylor shook his head as he guided the truck around another bend in the pitch-dark road. What was he *doing* out here?

It was the middle of the night, and he had to report for duty at eight in the morning down at Moose. He'd transferred to Grand Teton National Park as a law enforcement ranger only a few weeks ago—it wouldn't make a good impression on his new boss to show up late, even if the chief ranger at his last station had given him a glowing recommendation.

And yet here he was, returning late from a weekend visit to his sister's place out in the Bighorn Mountains, and making himself even later by detouring past Sadie Madsen's ranch.

It wasn't like he was going to *see* her...or anything, for that matter, when it was this dark outside. But it'd been seven years since he'd moved away, and nearly as long since he'd worked up the courage to ask after her.

The familiar sense of guilt and regret pulled him down into his seat like gravity had just doubled. *Water under the bridge. Right, Lord?* He'd done what he thought was best at the time, and that was that. Even though he'd avoided coming back here at all costs, the National Park Service and his Heavenly Father had seen otherwise.

His mom had told him about Sadie's parents passing four years back. The news had been a punch in the gut. Dale and Cathy Madsen were good people, despite the angry last words he'd exchanged with her father. How had Sadie coped with their deaths? From what he'd heard, their loss wasn't the only hit the ranch had taken. But she had a foreman and hired hands to help run the operation, and she'd always been strong.

So, he would drive right on past Double M Ranch, make sure the sign and the rest of the place was still standing.

Prove to himself Sadie was a-okay without him and maybe relieve some of this nagging guilt in the process.

Landmarks didn't show up on a night like this, where the sliver of moon hung lower in the east than a cowboy's belt buckle. But navigating these roads was like riding a bike—it stuck with you even after years away. Past this endless stretch of pristine fence that marked the Diamond Ranch, then around the bend, and Sadie's ranch would be there on the left. Not nearly as big as her neighbor's, but some of the prettiest land this side of the Tetons.

He leaned forward in the seat, squinting out the windshield. Was that an orange glow on the horizon? Or had the town of Jackson grown so much he could see the lights from here?

Any thought of driving past evaporated as he guided the truck around the bend and the Double M Ranch gate came into view. The long gravel drive wrapped back between rolling hills until it reached the main house and the outbuildings. None of the structures were visible from here, but that orange glow was definitely coming from the ranch. Unless Sadie was recreating the Texas A&M Aggie Bonfire on her property, something was very wrong.

He tightened his grip on the wheel, slowing the truck just enough to make the left turn into the ranch without toppling his vehicle. Gravel kicked out from beneath the truck's tires as he steered up the long drive toward the main buildings. His stomach dropped as they came into view. The barn—

Its roof was a blazing inferno, with columns of smoke drifting upward to meet the stars.

Lord, please... There wasn't time to formulate words into a prayer as he slammed to a halt on the circle drive between the barn and the house. A horse whinnied nearby, running loose in the front yard of the main house. No one was out here. Where were the fire trucks? Or at least the ranch hands with water hoses? And Sadie?

He flung open the truck door and leaped out, then reached back inside for the phone sitting in the center console. Had anyone even called 9-1-1? After tapping the emergency call button on his cell, he dashed toward the exercise yard. There'd be a hose out there.

"9-1-1, what's your emergency?"

He relayed the information to the dispatcher, then realized that noises were coming from the barn—or was it from the other side? Horses whinnying. Thumping. An uneven cadence of hooves pounding the ground.

Black and brown masses moved at the edge of the fire's glow. At least some of the horses had gotten out and now roamed the paddock. But were more still trapped inside?

And where was Sadie?

"No sign of Sadie, the ranch owner. She might be trapped inside. I have to go," he said to the dispatcher.

"Wait, it's not—"

He ended the call without waiting for the warning. Of course, it wasn't safe. But he wasn't about to just stand here and let Sadie or her animals die. After vaulting over the paddock fence, he sprinted for the sliding doors. A metal rod had been stuffed through the door handles to lock them shut. Odd, but then maybe it was a last-minute fix when the regular lock broke?

The rod pulled loose without a fight, and after he chucked it aside, he yanked open one of the sliding doors. Smoke billowed out, but there was no sign of motion. He pulled the top of his T-shirt up over his mouth and nose, then flicked on the flashlight of his phone. One of the nearest stall doors was open—that must be how the horses got out. But where was Sadie?

Then the light snagged on the floor inside the stall with the open door, where the prone form of a woman lay unmoving. Her face was turned away from him, hidden behind the long blond hair that spread across the floor like glossy hay. But even after all these years, he recognized her immediately. *Sadie.*

He rushed toward her and stooped down, hoisting her up with one arm beneath her legs and the other supporting her back. Blood crusted her forehead and matted her hair on one side. *Please, Lord, let her be okay,* he prayed.

When he reached the door, he paused to glance back. The fire had consumed the roof at the far end, dropping burning timber down onto the hay bales stored below. Flames gobbled up the dry hay, leaping from one bale to the next. Soon the whole place would go up. But there was no other sign of movement. Sadie must've gotten all the horses out.

Jesse turned his back on the inferno and carried her across the exercise paddock to the grass on the far side, a safe distance from the flames. With the bare gravel surrounding the building and nothing more than a light breeze tonight, at least the fire wouldn't spread. He laid her gently on the ground.

He pressed two fingers to her neck, relieved to feel a pulse. Breath wafted across his hand when he held it in front of her mouth. "Sadie? Can you hear me?"

She groaned, shifting her weight, but her eyes didn't open.

With a crash, more timbers collapsed inside the barn. He jerked around, gaping as the fire engulfed the structure like a huge red mouth.

The faint sound of sirens reached his ears as he crouched next to Sadie. Her eyes fluttered open, widening as she took in the blazing inferno consuming her barn. Orange light flickered against her dark irises as she stared unblinking.

"Sadie?" His voice came out rough, and he cleared his throat. "Hey, you okay?"

"My horses… I tried to…get them, but Bonnie…"

"It's okay. They're in the paddock on the side, except for a couple loose in the yard. I'll make sure they're safe." Eventually. Once the immediate emergency had been dealt with, and she was safe.

"My barn is burning down, isn't it?" The words were so soft, he almost didn't hear them.

Suddenly his throat felt unbearably tight. He nodded, even though she wasn't looking at him.

She didn't seem to expect an answer. "It's pretty, isn't it? The fire? Too bad it's so destructive. Why is this happening to me?" Her eyes drifted shut again, sending a jolt of alarm spiking through his system.

Every bit of first aid training felt suddenly useless. This wasn't some park visitor who'd gotten injured on a hike— this was Sadie Madsen, the only woman he'd ever loved.

"Sadie? Hey, you need to stay awake." In the direction of the ranch entrance, red and blue lights flashed against the black night over one of the hills. "Help is coming." He reached for her, stopping just shy of touching her when her eyes opened again.

She turned toward him. Her forehead creased as she studied him. From the slightly unfocused look in her eyes, she'd suffered blunt-force trauma along with whatever had caused the bleeding on her forehead. Did she even recognize him?

"Jesse Taylor?" she said faintly. "You broke my heart." She lifted her hand, her fingers swaying in front of his face. "Good thing you're not real."

Definitely a head injury. There's no way the Sadie he knew would talk to him that calmly, after what had happened. He caught her hand in his, then laid her arm gently back on the ground. Her skin was cold and clammy, like she might be going into shock. There was a spare blanket in his truck, but the emergency vehicles were almost here, and he didn't want to leave her. So he settled for removing his flannel shirt from over his black undershirt and laying it on top of her.

Two fire trucks pulled in, followed by a police cruiser. Firefighters in black-and-yellow gear spilled out and went to work hooking up hoses to the pumper engine. Jesse stood up, waving, and a police officer jogged over to him with a first aid kit.

"She's conscious and appears to be stable," Jesse said. "Might have suffered a TBI, though."

The man flipped on a flashlight and shined it at Sadie's face. She blinked, turning away. He let the light linger on the matted blood in her hair, then clicked it off. "EMS should be here in five minutes. How about you, sir? Are you all right?"

"Yes, I just got here a few minutes ago when I spotted the fire from the road."

By the time an ambulance arrived, the firefighters had two hoses going, one connected to a tank on the engine and the other pulling from a creek that ran a short distance from the house. The fire was retreating rather than spreading, and blackened timbers jutted out from the near end of the barn in its wake.

Medics pulled out a stretcher and jogged over to where Jesse waited with Sadie. She hadn't said anything else—just lay there watching the firefighters work.

The barn was beyond saving now, but maybe there'd still be salvageable equipment inside or some timbers that could be reused. His chest ached as he thought about how hard this would be for her. From what little he'd seen, the barn appeared to be a newer structure. Less than five years, if he had to guess.

His mother, who still lived in Jackson, had sent him enough unasked-for updates over the years that he knew Sadie had had a rough time. First her parents' deaths, and then stories here and there about losses hitting the ranch. This fire would be yet another financial hit.

What had caused it? And where was the ranch foreman or any of the hands? When they were kids, the place had always been overflowing with cowboys.

As the EMTs hoisted the stretcher, Sadie reached out toward him. "Kip, my dog—he's still in the house," she said around what sounded like a mouthful of gravel.

He took her hand again, squeezing gently. She'd probably chew him out once she recovered, but for now he'd take the peace offering. "I'm going to take care of him, okay? Don't you worry about anything. I'll swing by the hospital as soon as I can."

Her fingers slid out of his as the EMTs carried the stretcher to the waiting ambulance. *Please be with her, Lord.* He hated for her to be alone at the hospital, but he needed to make sure her horses were secure and the fire was put out. There'd be time to process emotions later.

A police officer was examining something on the ground beside the barn doors. Jesse jogged over. The man's flashlight illuminated the metal rod that Jesse had pulled out of the door handles.

A horrifying thought struck him like a backhanded slap.

When he'd removed that bar, he'd figured Sadie was using it as a makeshift lock. But not if she was *inside* the barn...unless she'd entered through a different door. Was that likely?

"Evening, Officer," he said, crouching down nearby. "I'm Jesse Taylor, law enforcement ranger in Teton."

"Deputy Griggs, Teton County Sheriff's Department." He offered a hand, and Jesse shook it. "You pulled the victim out of the barn?"

He winced at the word *victim* in connection with Sadie. Suddenly it felt like decades since they'd been engaged. "Yes, sir. In fact, that metal bar was stuck through the door handles."

The officer frowned, then pulled a pair of gloves from his pocket. "Better get this dusted then. We'll get a team out here in the morning to evaluate the structure for potential cause, and we'll need to get an official statement from you and Ms. Madsen."

Jesse nodded. "Happy to help. I'm going to secure things here, then I'll head to the hospital to check on her." And notify his boss there was no way he'd make it in for his shift. He couldn't leave Sadie stranded at the hospital.

He stood, scanning the charred shell that remained of the barn. On this end, the sliding doors on their runners were still standing. The only smaller doors were around the sides, where the horse stalls had Dutch doors opening out into the exercise paddocks.

A light still gleamed through one of the house's windows. How had she known about the fire? Was the barn rigged with an alarm? No doubt she'd left the door un-locked—after he found her dog, maybe he could lock up for her.

The front door was still ajar when he nudged it open. Barking greeted him, and he peered in to see a large collie sitting a few feet from the door.

He frowned. "Duke?"

The dog whined. No, Sadie had called him Kip. And the top of his ears tipped over, where Duke's had been upright. Nor was there enough black on the muzzle. Besides—he did a little math in his head—Duke would be nineteen years old by now, impossibly old for a dog.

Time took its toll on everything. He gritted his teeth as a wave of regret washed over him, then he crouched and held out his hand. "Hey, Kip. I'm a friend of Sadie's."

That was a stretch, but Kip rose from his haunches and, after sniffing Jesse's hand, wagged his tail and let Jesse scratch behind his ears. At least Sadie's *dog* liked him. He stood, surveying the inside of the still house.

A rifle, loaded and ready, sat propped in the umbrella stand. He picked it up and slid the safety back into place. Best to put this away before any accidents happened. A light was on farther inside, where Dale's office used to be.

The rest of the house was dark and quiet as he passed through with Kip following at his heels. When he reached the office, he slid the rifle back into the gun safe and closed the door. An open ledger lay on the desk, with the lamp on over it. He glanced briefly at it—Sadie's accounts for the ranch. She must've been up late, poring over these pages, when something alerted her to the fire. Nothing else seemed out of place, so he flipped off the light and used his phone's flashlight to navigate back to the front door.

Walking through the place felt unnervingly familiar, and yet…completely different. Some of the same wall decor and furniture pieces were still here, like that umbrella stand that had stood next to the front door for decades. Wrapped in memories. But the space felt emptier, somehow, without Mr. and Mrs. Madsen, and the heavy cinnamon candle scent Sadie's mom had favored was gone, replaced with something light and fresh.

He shook off the bittersweet mix of nostalgia and loss and turned for the door. Sadie's keys hung on a hook above the umbrella rack, so he grabbed the ring, flipped on the porch light and called the dog. "Come on, Kip, we've got to round up Sadie's horses and take them to the old barn."

After they were done, he'd take the dog along and leave him at his mom's in town until he knew how long Sadie would be in the hospital.

As he walked toward the exercise paddock near the charred shell of the barn, he mulled over what had happened. Sadie must've heard something that made her get up to check, then seen the fire. She'd left the gun and gone to the barn. What was her goal? Not to put the fire out, or she wouldn't have been inside. Maybe to free the horses?

Whatever her plans, he couldn't think of a single reason why she'd leave the sliding doors barred shut and enter through one of the stalls.

The police officer was still scanning the ground with his flashlight, talking into a radio. Jesse would have to wait for the official report to get more details, but he couldn't shake the thought that there was only one solid explanation for what had happened:

Somebody had trapped Sadie inside.

TWO

Jesse waited as the glass front doors of the hospital slid open, then headed straight for the emergency room. It had to be after three in the morning by now, and although weariness tugged at his muscles, he was still running strong on adrenaline. And that cup of coffee from a gas station. He'd crash later.

Kip had proved to be an excellent herder as they rounded up as many horses as he could find and took them to the lower level of Sadie's big pole barn. The place wasn't outfitted for horses anymore, but at least it would keep them safe and contained until the morning.

Sadie would be relieved to hear it—*if* she was okay. Worry gripped his insides, but he shook it off as he asked the receptionist in the ER where to find her.

"She's in room twelve," the woman responded. "Are you a relative?" She pointed to a sign over her shoulder. *Family members only outside of visiting hours.*

Jesse gritted his teeth, then pulled out his NPS badge. Looked like he had to play the I'm-an-officer card. "I'm in law enforcement. I need to ask Ms. Madsen some questions."

She squinted at his badge, then waved him on. Maybe

it wasn't strictly necessary to carry his badge off duty, but you never knew when it would come in handy.

Sadie's room lights were dimmed, and she appeared to be sleeping when he glanced through the window in the door. A nurse paused outside the room as she walked by with a chart. "Are you here to see Ms. Madsen?"

He nodded. "How is she?"

"She's doing well. Vitals are stable. She has bruising and a cut on her forehead, but nothing requiring stitches. Since she blacked out after the head injury, the doctor ordered a CT scan. If those results come back clear, she'll be able to go home."

"Thank you." He reached for the doorknob as the nurse walked away, pausing for a second before opening it. If Sadie was feeling better, closer to normal, she wasn't going to appreciate seeing him. The last thing he wanted to do was upset her, but he had to make sure she'd be safe after she left the hospital. Taking a deep breath, he turned the knob and slipped inside the room.

At the sound of the door opening, Sadie shifted on the bed, angling so she faced him. Recognition flashed in her lovely brown eyes, then they narrowed. "Please tell me I have a head injury, and you're just a hallucination. Because if that's really you, Jesse Taylor…"

The knot in his chest loosened at her soft drawl. Good— there was the opinionated woman he knew. *Thank You that she's doing better, Lord.*

He exhaled slowly, taking a few steps closer. "Sorry to disappoint you, but it's really me. Do you remember what happened?"

She let out an exasperated huff before spearing him with a pointed gaze. "When you dumped me and skipped town three weeks before our wedding? Yes, I remember very well." '

Okay, maybe he deserved that. "No, I mean tonight. At the ranch. The fire?"

This time she closed her eyes. Pain flashed across her face, and she nodded before looking at him again. "You got me out, didn't you?"

"Yeah." He gestured to a chair near the bed. "Mind if I sit? I'd like to ask you a few questions."

"It's a free country." She watched him as he dropped into the seat. "Your uncle—who I must say is just as charming now as he was when he was interfering with our relationship seven years ago—told me you're in law enforcement. I ran into him a few weeks ago at the grocery store. Teton National Park, right?"

He held back a sigh. His mother's brother, Uncle Rob, had taken his mother and Jesse under his wing when Jesse's father died. Jesse had been twelve at the time, and his older sister had already moved out for college. As much as he appreciated Rob's help, especially his continued care for his mother, sometimes he wished there were still a couple states between the two of them. Rob had spent the six years until he left for college questioning every one of Jesse's decisions and making sure he knew he'd never be good enough. Too rough around the edges, too outdoorsy, not enough ambition.

"You sure you want to wear that outfit to the dance, kid?"

"I'd take business instead of AP biology, if I were you."

"Guess you should've spent more time studying and less time hiking, don't you think?"

It'd taken years to erase Rob's voice from his mind.

No one made him feel inadequate like Uncle Rob—except maybe Sadie's father. He swallowed the sour taste rising in his throat.

"Yes, Teton. I just moved back. Wasn't exactly planning on it…" He let the words trail away because this was off topic, too. "Anyway, I happened to drive by your ranch on my way home from my sister's last night, and I saw the fire from the road. Can you tell me what happened?"

She cupped her hands over her face, then reached for the control panel on the side of her bed. "Guess I'd better sit up." As the bed raised, she twisted, trying to adjust the pillows.

Jesse jumped up, moving them higher behind her back.

She gave him a wan smile. Even with her blond hair hanging limp over her shoulders and the bandage on her head, she was just as beautiful as he remembered.

"Thanks," she said, and he retreated to his seat. "I couldn't sleep. I was working in the office, close to midnight, when I heard the horses. I thought at first it was a wolf near the barn, but then I saw the flames."

That explained the rifle. "Do you know what started it?"

She shook her head, but one hand flexed, squeezing the sheet with a death grip. "I don't keep anything more flammable than hay in there. And there wasn't any lightning. My security camera system went down last year, so we may never know." Her mouth twisted, and something unreadable flashed in her eyes. "Anyway, the fire hadn't spread far yet, so I ran inside to let the horses out of their stalls."

"Did you enter through one of the outer stall doors?"

"No, through the main doors. The sliding ones. But when I got to the far end and released the last two horses, we couldn't get back out. The doors were stuck. I managed to get one of the stall doors open, but the horses panicked and knocked into me, and I must've hit my head." She touched her bandaged forehead gingerly. "Then I woke up outside."

Her words weighed down his chest like a ton of bricks. She'd entered through those sliding doors. Someone *else* had locked her inside. He balled a hand into a fist. How was he going to tell her what he'd found without frightening her?

"What is it?"

He shook his head.

"Out with it, Jesse. Don't just sit there staring at me like a guppy. I'm a big girl, I can handle it."

He slammed his mouth shut, fighting to keep a smile off his lips. She'd always been able to read him like an open book. Apparently, some things didn't change with time. "Sorry, Sadie. I just… When I got there, the sliding doors were shut. With a metal bar crammed through the handles. That's why you couldn't get out."

Her mouth went slack. "Somebody locked me inside."

"It looks that way. Can you think of anybody who might have something against you?" He frowned. "And where was your ranch foreman? Or any of the hands? Why were you all alone?"

She stared at the wall for several moments, clenching and unclenching a wad of the bed sheet on her lap. "My foreman and his wife are out of town, and none of the hands live on the ranch anymore. Trying to cut costs." She turned to him. "What about the horses? And Kip? Are they all right?"

"Kip helped me round up as many we could. And I left him at my mom's so he wouldn't be alone."

"Thanks." She exhaled, pressing a hand to her chest. "I guess I owe you after this."

"Right now, I just want to know you're safe and figure out what happened."

She nodded slowly, but her features drooped with something…sadness? Resignation? His gut twisted. She faced the fire all by herself last night, and now, in the hospital bed, she looked truly alone.

A knock sounded at the door, and the nurse entered, followed by a police officer. "I'm back to check your vitals again," she said brightly. "The doctor says your scans look good, so you should be able to go home soon."

Jesse rose from the chair to give her space and walked over to the officer.

The other man held out his hand. "Deputy Freeman, Teton County Sheriff's Department. I'm partnering with Deputy Griggs on this case."

Jesse shook his hand. "Jesse Taylor, law enforcement ranger at Grand Teton National Park. I'm an old friend of Sadie Madsen's. Happy to lend a hand any way I can."

When the nurse was finished, the deputy introduced himself to Sadie, took down her contact information and asked her to go over what had happened.

"Jesse told me about the doors being jammed shut," she said at the end of her recap.

Freeman nodded. "The lab is going to dust the bar for prints. The ground was too hard around the barn to leave any footprints, but we've got a team checking the creek bed. I'll keep Ranger Taylor updated on anything we find." He paused, studying Sadie. "Do you have any ideas who might have done it? Any enemies we should know about?"

Sadie pressed her fingertips to her forehead, massaging her skin. When she turned back to them, fire flashed in her dark eyes. "I realize how this is going to sound, but this isn't the first incident on the ranch."

"What do you mean?" Jesse frowned.

"We've had a spell of trouble for years that I chalked up to bad circumstances, like broken fences and sick cattle. And all the while I've been getting purchase offers from potential buyers. But then after I had a geologist come evaluate the land two months ago, it's like the entire world has figured out there might be oil underneath the Double M, and they're doubling down on their offers. Calling. Sending realtors. Then one of my ATV brake lines was cut, and a hay bale fell on my back—" She cut off, rubbing her shoulder for a moment, as the deputy scribbled on a notepad. "And now this."

Oil? Sadie was thinking about drilling on the Double M? Sure, it might yield a boatload of cash, but a rig on that pristine land… He cracked his knuckles. His opinion didn't matter anyway.

Freeman paused, his pencil hovering above the paper. "Who's been making offers? Can you give me names?"

Sadie nodded. "There's Amos Johnson, my neighbor. He owns the Diamond Ranch. He's been looking to expand his operation for years, and now he bought the land on the other side of me."

"Terrence and RaeAnne's?" Jesse pictured the white-haired woman who'd invited them over for lemonade on the porch back when they were dating.

"RaeAnne passed, and Terrence opted to sell to Amos." The look she shot him was full of reproach, her meaning all too clear. *If you'd stuck around, you would know.*

He cleared his throat and glanced down, busying himself brushing long, crimped collie hairs off his black shirt.

"Amos has made a number of offers over the years," she said, "though they've gotten more—I don't know if *aggressive* is the right word. More like…desperate?—since he bought Terrence's land. It's clear he's got cash, and he's willing to spend it."

The deputy's pencil scratched across the paper. He paused, flipping the page. "Anyone else?"

She hesitated, glancing between them. "You know Stanley Fitz? The state senator who lives south of the Hole and has that huge ranch outside Pinedale?"

Both he and Freeman nodded.

"He's running for federal senator, isn't he?" Jesse asked. Uncle Rob had mentioned the man a few times—apparently, they were friendly. Leave it to his uncle to know everyone of consequence within a hundred-mile radius.

"He's been after my land for years. Since my parents were still alive. Making offers by mail, by phone, even sending realtors in person." She drew in a slow breath. "What if he heard about the oil?"

The deputy paused his note-taking and exchanged a glance with Jesse. His take on Sadie's idea was fairly obvious from the skeptical quirk to his eyebrows. She *had* just sustained a head injury… Was it possible she was just grasping at straws? It was obvious someone was after her, but Fitz seemed like a stretch. Why would he risk his position for more land?

"That's a serious accusation, Ms. Madsen," the deputy said.

She held up her hands. "I'm not accusing anybody. I'm merely suggesting. You're the one who asked. But it stands to reason that if I took enough financial hits, I might be more easily persuaded to sell. I didn't even list the fifteen plus oil companies who've sent offers to buy or lease the mineral rights."

Jesse frowned. "But if someone set fire to the barn to try to run you off your land, why would they lock you inside? How are you going to sell if you're—" He slammed his mouth shut before the awful word popped out. "Who gets the land if anything happens to you? Would it be easier for someone to buy?"

She shook her head. "It's tied up in a trust, but maybe they don't know that. Or maybe it was a scare tactic? They were planning on letting me out, but you arrived and frightened them off?"

No matter the reason, he didn't like this. At all. Sadie had nearly died. Sure, their history together was complicated and buried deep in the past, but that didn't mean he could witness her in this kind of danger and feel *nothing*.

The deputy flipped his notebook closed. "Thank you for answering my questions, Ms. Madsen. When you're up to it, I'd like a list of every individual or company that's made you an offer." He walked closer, holding out a booklet. "Here's some information about what happens next. You'll find our contact information and your case identification number inside. Feel free to call anytime. We'll keep you updated."

"Thank you." Sadie accepted the booklet and stared down at the cover. *A Guide for Victims of Crime*. Her shoulders hunched beneath the hospital gown, and she seemed to shrink.

Jesse's heart sank. Crime victims in the national parks were usually travelers, and the most common incidents were thefts or a rare assault. He'd take their statements, reassure them the matter would be investigated and send them on their way.

But the ranch was Sadie's home, and here she was, sitting in a hospital with a head injury and no family to take care of her. He shook the officer's hand again, then cracked his knuckles as the door opened and closed, leaving him alone with Sadie. It was a bad habit—he'd probably end up with arthritic hands—but it was the only way to contain the uncomfortable energy buzzing through his insides.

He had his job to get back to, and Sadie's problems weren't his. She might not even *want* his help after how badly he'd failed her last time. But he'd changed over the years, and he didn't know how to sit back and let her fend for herself. Not in a situation like this.

What if the perpetrator returned to finish the job?

"Thank you again for your help," she said as soon as they were alone. Her tone almost sounded like a dismissal, which would've been humorous coming from someone in her position if he didn't know how stubborn she could be. "I'll call someone to get a ride home and then stop by your mom's for Kip."

The last traces of indecision warring in his chest vanished as he surveyed her. Dark circles popped under her eyes like bruises smudging her pale skin. Whether she wanted to admit it or not, Sadie needed help. He was right here, and he could make himself available. It was as simple as that.

"No, Sadie, I can take you home. Keep an eye on things and make sure you're safe until your foreman gets back." After what he'd put her through so many years ago, it was the least he could do. "Until the police know more, I don't feel comfortable leaving you alone."

* * *

Sadie wasn't sure she'd heard him correctly. The only reason her head wasn't splitting in two was because they'd pumped her full of ibuprofen, so maybe her ears weren't working.

Jesse had smashed her heart and walked out of her life without warning, and he expected her to trust him now?

Her gaze snapped to his. "Hold up. Seven years ago, you left. And now suddenly you're here, and you think you can just play the hero and save me?"

He stared without flinching. "That's exactly what I think, but only because you need help." His eyes were still the same color as a glacial lake. Light blue and piercing. He wore his dark hair shorter now, and his rugged jawline was concealed beneath facial hair that walked the fence between week-old scruff and a full beard. He'd added muscle, too, and tiny lines fanned out from his eyes, erasing the boyish features of his college days. Jesse had grown into a man, and unfortunately, he was even more infuriatingly handsome than ever.

"I don't think so." She forced her tight lips into a fake smile. Just because he had saved her life didn't mean he got any say in what happened now. "Zeke and Lottie will be back tomorrow afternoon, and my friend Katrina can give me a ride home. The ranch hands will be out in the south pasture by sunup. I'll hardly be alone. And in case you hadn't noticed, I've got plenty to do at the ranch without you getting underfoot."

Jesse folded his arms across his chest and leaned back against the wall, studying her until she felt like squirming beneath the starchy hospital sheet. Just when she couldn't take the silence any longer, he pushed off the wall and eased into the chair next to her. "Look, Sadie, I'm sorry about how things ended between us. I didn't handle it well."

She scoffed. *That* was the understatement of the century.

He pinned her with his steady gaze. "But right now, you're just being stubborn, and we both know it. If you don't let me drive you home, I'm going to follow you anyway to make sure you stay safe until the Nelsons return. We both know that south pasture is miles from the main house. Your ranch hands won't be anywhere near you. Besides, it's 4:00 a.m. Your friend will thank me."

His gaze stayed locked on hers, ice cool and determined.

She stared him down for a few seconds longer, but her head still ached, and exhaustion threatened to strip away whatever resolve she had left. Maybe it was better to let him have his way. This once.

"Fine," she grumbled. "But only because we have to get Kip." And Katrina would probably panic when she heard about the fire—Sadie could put off that conversation until her head didn't hurt quite so much.

The brief victory smile that flashed across his face almost made her swallow her words, but he reined his features back to neutral almost instantly.

As if on cue, a knock sounded at the door, and the doctor entered, followed by the nurse who'd examined her earlier.

"How are you feeling?" the doctor asked as the nurse checked her vitals again.

"Better," she said. "I still have a headache, but nothing like before. And the brain fog is gone." She could only vaguely remember what happened back at the ranch—Jesse waking her up outside the barn, the smoke in the air, the shrieking of the sirens. Hopefully she hadn't said anything too embarrassing.

"Good." The doctor made a few notes on her chart. "Your CT scan looks good. No signs of further damage, though with head injuries sometimes it can take a few days before the full extent is known. You'll need to take it easy. No straining yourself, okay?"

This ranch owner wasn't exactly wealthy enough to sit around on her backside doing nothing. But she nodded, making sure to look compliant. Then the doctor and nurse stepped outside with Jesse—probably issuing more discharge instructions she wouldn't want to follow—while she changed out of the oversize hospital gown and back into her own clothes.

Jesse's flannel shirt lay at the bottom of the stack the nurse had saved for her. Thick and soft and carrying the faintest scent of musky leather and cedar. She stopped herself seconds before she would've pressed it to her face.

Better to stuff that back into the plastic sack and pretend she'd never seen it.

Jesse was waiting alone outside her door by the time she finished changing. She felt laid bare and vulnerable, with no cell phone, no wallet, nothing but the dirt-streaked lounge pants and T-shirt she'd been wearing before bed. No choice but to accept help from the man who'd broken her heart—

No, enough of that. She needed to think of him the same as she would any other man.

"Got everything?" he asked.

She held out the bag containing his shirt. "Here's your flannel back. Thanks for letting me borrow it." Not that she'd exactly asked.

"Sure." As he took it, his warm fingers brushed lightly against her cold ones. An unexpected jolt of awareness sizzled up her skin, and she jerked back.

Surprise flashed across his face, as if he'd felt it, too, but thankfully he didn't say anything.

Awkward. The sooner she could get away from him, the better.

She followed him as he led the way out of the hospital and to his truck, a black Dodge Ram that couldn't be more than a few years old. Looked like he was doing well for himself.

"Nice truck," she said, trying to keep the bitter edge out of her tone. *Love one another, as I have loved you.* Jesus's words from the Gospel of John flew into her mind. What was wrong with her? This wasn't how God wanted her to treat others—even if they had hurt her.

"Thanks." He opened the passenger door and offered a hand to help her up, but she wasn't falling for that again. Instead, she grabbed the door handle and pulled herself inside the cab. "I bought it used a few months ago when I found out they'd assigned me to Teton."

She clicked her seat belt into place as he walked around to the driver side and climbed in. "So, park rangers don't choose where they go?"

"Not really. We can make requests. I put my name in for Glacier, but they needed me here." He started the truck and pulled out of the hospital lot.

Huh. Coming back here hadn't been his choice. She chewed silently on that piece of information as they headed west toward the center of Jackson.

The town was small, and no traffic blocked their way at this hour, so only a few minutes later he pulled to a stop in front of a row of businesses. She'd always thought the Western-themed storefronts here were charming, with their log-and-stone facades and big neon signs in the shapes of cowboys and boots.

"Mom still has her apartment over Bert's," Jesse said, then cleared his throat. Maybe he felt as uncomfortable about this unplanned reunion as she did. He shut off the engine, and they climbed out.

"Best coffee in town." Sadie followed him into a narrow alley that led behind the darkened coffee shop, then up the flight of stairs to the apartment above.

The way the steps creaked, the musty smell of the air, the feel of the railing beneath her hand... How many times had she come here with Jesse for a meal after church or just to drop by and say hi after they'd strolled the town square on a Friday night? And yet it had been *years* since those days. Everything about it felt unnervingly familiar and yet different, like she'd slipped through a looking glass and turned into Alice in Wonderland.

Jesse knocked softly, and a moment later, Lisa Taylor pulled the door open. The petite older woman was swimming in a thick oversize fleece bathrobe, her gray hair pulled back into a loose bun. Her face split into a wide grin when she saw Sadie, crinkling the skin around her eyes. "Why, Sadie Madsen, you poor thing. Come here."

She pulled Sadie into a hug, wrapping her in the soft scent of vanilla musk. They'd run into each other every now and then over the years, and Lisa had always been kind to her. Maybe the older woman knew their breakup had been entirely her son's fault.

"Mom," Jesse said gently, "she's been injured, remember?"

"Of course." Lisa drew back and settled for taking Sadie's arm as she steered her inside. "You just lie there on the sofa while I make you a cup of tea."

"Oh, we can't, Mrs. Taylor, but thank you." Sadie's head

was aching again, and all she wanted was to get Kip and go home. "I need to get back to the ranch."

"We're just here to get Kip, Mom."

At their voices, Kip came running over from wherever he'd been sleeping. His tail wagged and he squirmed with happiness, licking Sadie's hand.

She crouched down and pulled him into a hug, blinking back the moisture in her eyes. "Hey, boy!"

Thank You for protecting him, Lord. Kip had been her faithful companion for years, ever since her parents had passed. What would she do without him? "Jesse's going to take us home." She turned to Lisa. "Thank you for taking care of him while I was in the hospital."

Jesse looked on, his expression shuttered. What was going through his mind? Surely, he had never expected the three of them to be together like this again, either.

"Anytime, Sadie." Lisa smiled. "Anything for you."

The dog trotted down the steps with Sadie as they walked out to Jesse's truck. Kip waited next to her while he unlocked the vehicle.

"I noticed he doesn't jump in," Jesse said as he opened the rear passenger door.

"After Duke tore his ACL, I trained Kip not to. I've got a step for him in my truck." She moved closer and crouched to pick up the heavy dog, but Jesse touched her shoulder.

"Let me," he said. "You shouldn't be straining yourself. And I'm sorry to hear about Duke. He was a good dog."

Too exhausted to argue, she stepped aside. Jesse leaned down, slid his arms beneath Kip and lifted the heavy collie. Veins stood out against his taut arm muscles. He'd bulked up since she'd last seen him as a twenty-two-year-old. Not in a power-lifter kind of way, but in an "I can easily lift your seventy-pound dog" kind of way. It was hard to smother her sense of appreciation for his strength.

By the time they'd loaded Kip into the truck's back seat and pulled away from the curb, the lights had kicked on in Bert's coffee shop. The city's early risers were waking up.

Exhaustion clawed at Sadie, dragging her deeper into the seat. Before long, the ride would be over, and she'd have to face the carnage that used to be her new horse barn. There'd be the missing horses to round up and tend, the insurance company to call, more numbers to crunch. She'd have to go over it all again with Zeke and Lottie. Her head throbbed just thinking about it.

"How many horses did you find?" she asked. Better to know what to expect.

He was silent for a moment, as if counting in his head. "Eight, I think?"

That left four if his count was right. "What about the big black stallion?" The words came out tight, even though she tried to keep her tone even.

"I don't think so."

Her heart sank. It'd be just like Orion to run off and injure himself in the creek bed. That horse seemed to know he and his stud fees were the only reason she'd been able to keep things afloat lately.

"It's going to be okay." Jesse's low voice cut through her dismal thoughts. "I know it doesn't feel like it right now, but God is in control, and He's looking out for you."

Tears pricked her eyes, and she quickly blinked them away. Jesse was the last person she wanted to hear words of comfort from. The fact he was right made her even angrier.

"I know that," she mumbled as soon as she could trust her voice. Then she twisted away from him, turning toward the window. "It's just easier to *say* it to someone in a bad situation than to *be* the person in the bad situation." She leaned her head back and closed her eyes. Right now, she just needed a little rest.

She woke up a short time later as the truck jostled over a cattle grate on the road. In the east, the sky had faded from black to milky twilight like denim jeans that had been washed too many times.

Headlights pierced the front windshield, making her blink. "Turn off your brights already, buddy," she muttered, angling her body toward the passenger window. She let her eyes drift shut again, wishing the sweet oblivion of sleep could chase away reality a little longer.

Jesse chuckled. The low and easy sound tugged uncomfortably at her chest. "Almost home, sleepyhead—"

His truck horn blared as he slammed on the brakes.

Sadie's eyes flew open as her body slung forward in the seat. The belt locked in a stranglehold across her shoulder and waist. Her vision filled with the blinding twin orbs of approaching headlights.

The oncoming vehicle had crossed the double yellow line and was barreling straight toward them.

THREE

She screamed, clutching for the handle above the passenger door, as Jesse yelled, "Hold on!" In the back seat, Kip barked. *Protect him, Lord!*

It was like a game of chicken, only they weren't on farm tractors—they were in a truck going way too fast on a country road, with nowhere to bail. As the other vehicle bore down on them, Sadie squeezed her eyes shut.

Suddenly the truck lurched to the side, shuddering and bouncing half on the shoulder and half on grass, as the other vehicle shot past. She had the sense to spin in her seat and glance back at it. Dark blue or black SUV, Wyoming plates, but she couldn't make out the numbers as it sped away.

As she caught her breath, she glanced down at Kip. The collie had slid off the bench seat and now sat wedged on the floor behind her. He licked her hand when she reached for him, then jumped back onto the seat with unhindered movement. A valve released in her chest. He was okay.

Jesse guided the truck back up onto the shoulder and slowed to a stop, glancing in his rearview mirror. Then he turned to her, letting out a slow breath. His blue eyes skimmed across the seat belt, as if to make sure it had held, then up to her face. "You all right?"

She nodded, more to convince herself than to answer. "Yeah, I'm fine." *Fine.* Because it was normal now for her life to be in danger. A sigh shuddered out of her.

Jesse's gaze lingered, concern crinkling his forehead, but she pressed her lips together and straightened in her seat.

"Right now, I just want to get home. We can notify the deputy when we get back. I didn't catch the plates, just that it was a dark SUV."

Kip whined as if to punctuate her words.

Jesse reached a hand back to the dog, then turned forward and eased the truck back onto the road. He kept glancing in the rearview mirror, as if he expected the SUV to make a reappearance, but the road behind them remained empty.

As they rolled down the ranch's gravel drive, the first rays of dawn bathed the land in glistening gold and orange. The hulking, blackened skeleton of the barn made her wince. It was even worse than she'd imagined—a total loss. She hated to imagine how much her insurance rates would go up. Would any of the tack or other gear inside be salvageable?

And then there was the small matter of someone locking her inside…

A chill sneaked its way up her back, making goose bumps pop on her arms. It'd been easy to ignore that detail back in the hospital where she was safe, but now that she'd returned, the memory of being trapped hit her full force. And that vehicle that had tried to run them off the road—where had it come from?

Here?

She shivered, suddenly glad that she wasn't alone.

Jesse put the truck in Park and shut off the engine, then

held up a hand. "Wait here a minute, okay? I want to make sure no one else is lurking around."

"Do you think that SUV…" The words stuck in her throat like a bite of potato too dry to swallow.

He nodded as if he'd read her mind. He'd always had a knack for knowing what she was thinking. "Yes, it might have come from here." His gaze softened. "Unless it was someone who fell asleep at the wheel. Could've been coincidence." He didn't look like he believed it, though.

She waited a few endless minutes as he got out of the truck and surveyed the property, walking a short distance beyond the house to check its exterior and down the road leading to the other outbuildings.

When he came back, he shook his head. "I didn't see anything else out of place. Let's be cautious, though, okay?"

She nodded, then busied herself getting out and opening Kip's door. "Do you mind helping him out? He's not supposed to jump down, either. I'll call Zeke first thing. The sooner he gets back, the sooner you can leave."

Something flickered in his expression, but she ignored it. Jesse Taylor had done enough already. He didn't want to be here any more than she wanted him hanging around.

"Here's your key," he said, pressing a key chain into her palm after he walked around to her side of the truck. "I locked the house before I left last night."

Something else to thank him for. But all she could manage was a tight nod as he gently cradled Kip, then set him on the ground. She turned to the house, and his boots crunched on the gravel behind her as he followed, Kip trotting along next to him.

She twisted the key in the lock and pushed open the heavy oak door. Golden sunlight shot into the entryway, illuminating something white lying on the inside doormat. An envelope. Sadie stooped to pick it up, her head throbbing with the motion.

"What is it?" Jesse asked from behind her.

She turned, flashing the unmarked business-size envelope, then ran her thumb beneath the flap. A single sheet of paper was tucked inside, with an ad for a local real estate agency and words cut from glossy magazine paper taped to it.

Should've listed the place when you had the chance, Sadie.

She braced an arm against the doorframe as her head swirled. Who had slid this under her door? Whoever was driving that SUV? If only she'd sprung for new security cameras. Yes, she'd told the officer about Amos Johnson and Stanley Fitz and all the other unrelenting offers to buy the ranch, but she hadn't truly believed someone would threaten her into selling. Had she?

"Sadie?" Alarm rang in Jesse's voice. She moved aside to let him in. Kip followed, trotting over to his dog bed beside the big stone hearth. After closing the door behind them, she walked to one of the oversized leather armchairs and collapsed into it.

"Someone left this." She waved the letter at him.

He took it from her and sat on the nearby sofa. When he lifted his gaze to hers, anger flashed in his eyes. "It wasn't here when I locked your door. They came back to your house after the police left. Or they never left. It must've been whoever tried to run us off the road." He set the letter on the coffee table and pulled out his phone. "I'm calling Deputy Griggs. He can add this to their evidence when he gets here."

"While you do that, I'm going to clean up." She gestured at the dirt smears on her pants. What she needed was a few moments alone to pull herself together and fight off this sense of being completely overwhelmed.

Tears burned her eyes as she escaped into her bedroom and pulled her favorite pair of jeans out of a drawer. Then she grabbed her softest button-down shirt from the closet, along with a hooded jacket to fight off the early morning chill. Comfort was important on a day like this, when she wasn't sure she was strong enough to meet its demands.

By the time she washed her face, dressed and ran a brush through her tangled hair, she felt almost human again. She prodded gently at the gauze still taped to her forehead. It hadn't needed stitches, but a knot had already started to form. The medical tape was annoying, but it would be better to leave the wound covered for now.

As she returned to the living room, the scent of freshly brewing coffee filled the air. She found Jesse in the kitchen, leaning against the big island countertop as he watched the coffee drip through the coffeemaker. He'd put his flannel shirt back on, highlighting his broad shoulders and leaving a subtle scent of leather whenever he moved.

His gaze swept over her, stalling on her face. From the slight frown to his lips, he was still worried. "You're paler than a jackrabbit in winter. You should rest. I can call your foreman and tend the horses."

For a moment she imagined giving in—what it would be like to fall into her soft bed and sleep for hours while she let all these problems belong to someone else—but then she shook her head. "It's my ranch. I'm not going to slough off

Kellie VanHorn   47

the responsibilities onto someone else." Especially someone who'd already proven himself untrustworthy.

His shoulders slumped as if he'd read her mind.

Guilt prickled beneath her skin, but she let it go. Even
if she was being too harsh, didn't he deserve it after aban-
doning her? At the very least, she had to keep her guard up
around him. After all, Jesse would be back out of her life
within hours. Sooner, if Zeke got here faster. That's the way
life was—people came and went, and if she wanted to make
sure the ranch kept going, the responsibility fell squarely
on her shoulders. Counting on someone else would only
lead to disappointment. Hadn't Jesse proven that? And the
deaths of her parents?

She accepted a steaming mug of coffee when he handed
it to her, then stirred in a scoop of sugar. "Thanks. What
did the police say?"

"Deputy Griggs will be back out this morning, and he'll
collect the letter then. They're still waiting on lab results
for the metal bar. The team also found a partial footprint
down near the creek, but they haven't identified who it
might belong to."

"If the police will be here, you don't need to stay." She
took a sip of the scalding liquid, looking at him over the
rim of the cup.

But he shook his head. "They've got an investigation to
manage. They're not going to be able to help you like I can."

He'd been so quick to run last time, splitting from town
with practically no warning. Just a stop by her house with
his car fully packed. He'd caught her out in the old barn
mucking the stalls. She'd been knee-deep in dirty hay when
he appeared in front of her, breathless, spewing out non-
sense about how he wasn't right for her, how he was leaving

for a new job in another state with the National Park Service that very minute. In her state of shock, she'd barely been able to argue with him, much less get him to tell her the real reason he was going. Later, when she'd had a chance to recover, she'd called him, but he had refused to explain. When she'd tried again, he never picked up. Never called back. Until one day, she gave up.

So why was he sticking around now? Was this his attempt to make amends? Ha, as if that was possible.

"Fine, have it your way." She pointed at the fridge. "There's some leftover bacon and eggs if you're hungry. I'm going to call Zeke, and then we'll have to find the missing horses and get the others settled into the old barn. Might need to help the hands with the cattle, too. I'm down to only Cliff and the two Burton brothers."

"Won't they need the horses for work?"

She shook her head. "Dad switched to ATVs a few years after you left. More economical. If they took the back roads, they probably don't even know about the horse barn yet. I could call them to help, but why do that when you insist on sticking around anyway?"

After shooting him a falsely sweet smile, she pulled up Zeke Nelson's number on her phone. The call connected on the second ring. He and his wife were having a lovely visit with their new grandbaby, but as soon as he heard what'd happened, Zeke said they'd head out right away. They were hours across the state, though, so she wouldn't expect them until early afternoon.

When she hung up the call, Jesse practically shoved a plate of food into her hands.

"You need to sit down and eat," he insisted.

"I don't have time to eat." She veered around him and

the delicious-smelling food. The clock on the microwave read 6:53 a.m. Late by ranch standards, especially in June.

"Please, Sadie." He trailed after her. "You've never been particularly good at taking care of yourself."

She stopped and whipped around. "Pretty sure you don't have any right to make judgments about me. I've been just fine on my own for seven years." The words popped out before she could stop them, but she kicked herself on the inside. She'd decided last night in the hospital room that she needed to let it go and treat him the way she'd treat any other acquaintance.

Not to mention the statement wasn't *entirely* true. Clearly, she wasn't fine, given all these attacks on her and the ranch.

"Okay, then." He set the plate on the table with a soft clatter. "I already ate, so I'll go start on the horses." After draining the rest of his coffee, he put the mug into the dishwasher. "While you were getting changed, I called the number on the letter. For the real estate office?"

"I'm not listing this place." She winced at the volume of her words. As if she would *ever* let someone threaten her into selling.

He held up both hands. "I know, but I figured we should see if it was a legitimate business."

"And…?" Her stomach growled, and she reluctantly lifted the plate he'd offered her, digging into the cheesy scrambled eggs. Had he added more cheese? These were good. Or maybe she was just starving.

Or both.

"It's a legit agency in Jackson, at least according to their voice mail. They weren't open yet, of course, but they probably pay for ads in all the tourist magazines. Rich folks always want vacation homes in the Hole."

She finished chewing a bite of egg. "So it's most likely a coincidence that whoever left the letter happened to pick them?"

He nodded. "But I'm sure the police will follow up. Maybe they'll find something."

After he'd gone outside, Sadie finished her coffee and cleaned up her dishes. Hopefully that letter was just an empty threat, but after what had happened with the barn, and then that car trying to run them off the road...she wasn't so sure.

She shivered, then shook off the unhelpful fears. No use dwelling on the what-ifs when there was plenty of work to be done.

"Kip? You coming?"

The collie lay curled up on his bed near the fireplace, exhausted after their late night. An ear twitched, but otherwise he ignored her.

"Have it your way, lazybones."

By the time she slipped her feet into her leather boots and made it outside, Jesse was nowhere in sight. At least the caffeine had kicked in, and the morning sun shone on her face, warming her skin. It felt good to be back outside, doing something she loved.

No doubt the police would get here soon, and with the evidence they collected, she'd be able to prove to her insurance company that the fire wasn't her fault. Everything was going to be all right.

The dull roar of cars passing by on the main road added to the morning sounds created by a chorus of birds. Any one of those vehicles could be the police. She'd go help round up the horses with Jesse and then check back later.

She walked around behind the main house, following the dirt road a short distance to the old barn. They still used the large structure to store equipment and hay. The lower level opened to the ground in the back, allowing easy access to house injured cattle when needed. For now, it would work for the horses.

"Cops get here yet?" Jesse appeared around the side of the barn carrying a coil of rope.

She shook her head. "I heard cars out on the road, though. You still remember how to rope a horse?"

One eyebrow lifted as he smirked at her. "Don't forget who won the junior rodeo roping competition back in sixth grade."

"That was before your uncle turned you into a city dweller. Just don't hurt my horses."

"I caught eight of them last night. In the dark." His lips twisted. "Of course, they were all already in the exercise paddock. And Kip did most of the work."

She smothered a grin. "That leaves four, including my prize stallion, Orion."

"Nope, two more. I already roped two this morning down near the bunkhouse." He threw a thumb over his shoulder toward the lower side of the barn.

Sadie walked a few paces and glanced down to see Echo and Butterscotch with their noses buried in feedbags. Beyond them, the other horses stood in their makeshift stalls, swatting flies with their tails and eating hay.

Not bad. She could give credit where it was due. "Hey, nice wor—"

An engine roared down the gravel drive toward the

house. She jogged lightly back to where Jesse stood with one hand shielding his eyes from the sun. A blinding glare reflected off the approaching vehicle's windshield in the distance until it disappeared behind the contour of the landscape as it neared the house.

Why were the cops tearing down her road like that?

Jesse shot a worried look her way—apparently, he was thinking the same thing. "I'd better go meet them," he said.

But before he'd taken two steps, a loud, sharp crack echoed through the air, followed by more in quick succession.

After a lifetime on a ranch, it was a sound she'd recognize anywhere.

Gunshots.

"Get to cover!" Jesse urged, taking Sadie by the hand and dragging her toward the barn. He counted four shots before the gun went silent. The sound had come from the other side of the main house, near the burnt shell of the barn.

Sadie pulled open the barn door, and they raced inside. Beneath their feet, the lower level was visible through gaps between the wood planks. The car engine roared again outside, tires squealing—and it sounded like it was heading in their direction.

"Here!" Sadie led the way to a corner near the door, then vanished into the shadows behind a tractor. He followed, tucking into the small space next to her. A row of tools—rakes and shovels and pitchforks—dangled against the wall on her other side.

"Who is it?" she whispered.

"I don't know, I couldn't tell because of the glare." But he couldn't think of any reason law enforcement would open fire—unless there was a threat.

The roar of the engine drew closer, then idled outside. A car door slammed. Next to him, Sadie sat hunched like a taut coil. Footsteps crunched across the dirt and gravel outside. Whoever it was, they were making no effort to be quiet. The car drove off.

As he watched, the dark silhouette of a man appeared on the floor in the patch of light shining through the door-frame. "Anybody in here?" the man called. His voice was rough, with an edge that made adrenaline fire through Jesse's veins. "I'm lookin' for Sadie Madsen. Just want to talk."

The shadow on the floor shifted as the man moved, revealing the outline of a gun in his right hand.

Just want to talk, huh?

Jesse's chest tightened, and his hand inched toward his waist before he remembered he was out of uniform and didn't have his own gun.

The man entered the barn, his boots echoing across the floor. From his position, all Jesse could see was a pair of faded blue jeans draped over worn cowboy boots.

A radio crackled at the man's waist. "Barts, you copy?" came a new voice. "She's not in the house. Just a dog that tried to bite me before I locked it up."

Sadie tensed beside him. He glanced at her, holding up his hand in a silent gesture. *Don't move.*

"Copy," the man named Barts replied. "I'm in the big barn. Warden's gonna check the outbuildings. Over."

So, there were at least three of them. Jesse didn't like those odds, especially when he was unarmed.

The man walked slowly forward, stopping every few steps to look both ways. When his feet turned in the direction of their corner, Jesse held his breath. *Please hide us from him, Lord.* If his eyes weren't adjusted, maybe the shadows would be enough.

The seconds ticked past in an eternity of painful stillness, until finally the feet moved again, heading deeper into the barn. Jesse watched the man's back, making mental notes as he vanished between rows of stacked hay bales. Approximately five foot ten, medium build, black long-sleeved shirt and a cowboy hat. Carrying a semiautomatic handgun.

While he and Sadie were trapped and unarmed. Could they wait it out, until the police arrived? Deputy Griggs would be here anytime now. But what if they'd been delayed for some reason?

Their best chance of survival was to get back to Jesse's truck and get off the ranch. But how to do that unnoticed?

He scanned the row of tools hanging on the wall behind Sadie. One of those pitchforks or shovels could be an excellent makeshift weapon, but they were piled so haphazardly on their hooks, grabbing one might cause the entire stack to fall. Might as well just use a loudspeaker to announce their location.

As if she'd been following his gaze, Sadie touched his arm and pointed at the wall over the tractor's back tire. A trench shovel hung from its handle alone on a hook. He'd have to stand up and reach for it over Sadie and the tire, but if he could do it quietly enough, he had a chance.

Bracing a hand on the back of the tractor, he shifted his weight and rose out of a crouch. Sadie shrank back to give him more space, leaning dangerously close to the dangling tools. Sweat slicked his palms as he stretched for the shovel. Just as his fingers grazed wood, one of the horses stomped on the ground level below, then nickered softly. Jesse froze.

The man stopped. "That you, Ms. Madsen?" he called from the far end of the barn. Silence reigned for a moment, then the footsteps started again, coming toward them. It was now or never.

Jesse closed his fingers around the wooden shaft and lifted the shovel off the hook with a tiny *clang* that made him wince. Then he dropped back into a crouch just as the man reemerged from the stacked bales.

The man paused, then stooped to stare at the floor as if looking through the gaps at the horses below. "You can't hide forever," he said. "This time we're going to finish the job."

Acid burned Jesse's throat. So they *had* intended to kill her in that fire. But why? How had Sadie gotten a target on her back? Was it just because they wanted her land?

The man reached for his waist and pulled out his radio. "Barts here. No sign of her yet, but I still have to check the lower level. You got anything?"

"Outbuildings are clear," a male voice responded.

"If she's in here, I'll flush her out," Barts said.

Jesse glanced at Sadie. Worry crinkled her forehead. He pointed at the door, raised both his hands and mouthed, *Is that the only way out?*

She frowned at him for a minute, then shook her head and gestured toward the other end of the barn. Must be another door down there—if it wasn't already locked.

Indecision racked his insides. A shovel was no match for a gun. If they hid here while the man went down to check the lower level, they might be able to escape out the other door. But they'd have to cross the floor right over his head without attracting his notice. And if he torched the place and then waited outside with his friends, they'd be trapped.

Neither option sounded good, but Jesse far preferred the idea of taking out one of the men and keeping their location secret from the others, rather than facing all three of them from inside a burning barn. He nudged Sadie, then pointed toward the space between the tractor tires. She was small enough to fit, and the wheel would offer some protection.

Her eyes widened, and she shook her head at him, then glanced at the man. Barts still stood a few yards away, tucking the radio back into his belt, but any minute now he'd walk out.

Jesse pointed again, more emphatically this time. Now was the wrong time for her to be stubborn.

Finally she nodded, though fear tracked across her features.

He scanned the ground around them, looking for something to create a distraction, then settled on a chunk of broken shaft from some old tool propped up in the corner. Leaning carefully behind Sadie, he reached for the handle. His fingers closed around wood, and he plucked it silently off the ground. After nodding at Sadie, he tossed it a few yards away, deeper into the barn.

It hit the wood floor with a *thunk* halfway between their hiding place and the closest stack of hay bales.

Barts spun around, raising the gun.

Jesse ducked deeper behind the tractor and tightened his grip on the shovel handle. He'd only have one chance to catch the man off guard.

Barts's footsteps echoed softly across the floor.

Jesse pressed against the tire, leaning forward just enough to watch as the man approached the nearest pole supporting the hay loft. A few more feet when his back was turned... *Now.*

Jesse sprang from his hiding place, winding up the shovel like it was a baseball bat as Sadie dove for the space between the tractor tires. Just as Barts turned, eyes widening, Jesse swung the blade.

Barts tried to duck, but his reaction time was too slow, and he took the full brunt of the hit on his left shoulder. He hit the deck with a loud *thump*, and the gun clattered across the floor.

Jesse tossed the shovel aside and lunged for the gun. He scooped it up and aimed at Barts before the man had time to recover. "Hands up," he ordered. "I'm in law enforcement with the National Park Service, and you're under arrest."

Sadie crawled out from beneath the tractor.

Barts's face burned red when he saw her, and he opened his mouth like he was about to yell for his pals.

"Don't even think about it," Jesse said. "Now, why don't you explain what you're doing on this ranch while she finds some twine to tie you up?"

Barts's upper lip twitched. "I don't have to tell you nothin'."

"You realize that's a double negative, don't you?" As much as Jesse would love to pry some answers out of the man, they needed to get out of here before his friends showed up.

"Here." Sadie walked up with a length of twine and a roll of duct tape. "So he can't alert the others."

"Good thinking." Jesse took the twine and handed Sadie the gun, then secured Barts and covered his mouth with tape. He and Sadie jogged over to the door, keeping behind the cover of the wall as they scanned the perimeter. There was no sign of movement, but a blue Ford Explorer—maybe the same SUV they'd encountered earlier that morning—

sat parked a few hundred yards away near the bunkhouse. He strained to catch the license plate number, but the vehicle's rear bumper was obscured by a bush.

"What now?" She sagged against the wall of the barn but snapped upright as soon as she realized he was watching her. Poor woman—she'd been through far too much in the last twelve hours, and they still weren't safe.

"We get to my truck and get out of here."

"What about Kip?" She bit her lip. "I can't just leave him."

"Both the police and your foreman are on the way here. He'll be okay. What matters is getting *you* out of here." Jesse led the way out the door. "Come on."

Crouching low with Barts's gun in his hand, he jogged along the side of the barn. When they reached the end, he darted out of the shadows, across the gravel road and over to a fence on the other side. It didn't provide much cover, but at least he felt less exposed. Another short dash across the lawn led them to the front corner of the main house.

A burly man paced back and forth a dozen feet from the front door, a gun in his hand. He looked like he'd easily clear six feet and two hundred and fifty pounds of muscle. Beyond him, the top of Jesse's truck was visible on the other side of a decorative boulder in the front yard.

He turned back to Sadie, who crouched between the wall and a bush. "Someone's out there. We've got to go around the other way." As they raced around the back of the house, the Explorer's engine fired up. It wouldn't be long before the other man—the one called Warden—returned. Had he figured out what they'd done to Barts?

Sadie's hair blew over her shoulders as she darted along the back wall of the house in front of him, dodging sagebrush and landscaping rocks and deck furniture. They'd just rounded the corner of the garage on the other end of the house when the Explorer drove past, stopping somewhere in the front. Sadie cast a worried look at him over her shoulder. He tugged her to a stop, listening.

Low voices drifted from the front of the house, but he couldn't make out what they were saying. The engine remained on, out of sight from where they stood next to one of the closed garage doors.

"I think that's the same SUV that ran us off the road," she whispered. "Where are the cops?"

"I don't know. I'll call them as soon as we're safe. Let's go." He led the way up to the front corner of the house, silently running through their options. His keys were in his pocket, ready to go, but how were they going to cross the distance between their hiding place and his truck without getting shot?

A tall, lanky man wearing blue jeans and a red flannel shirt—must be the one named Warden—had joined the burly guy guarding the front door. They were absorbed in conversation, the burly one gesticulating wildly and waving his gun. Warden pointed at the SUV where it sat on the gravel road with the driver's door open.

Good—if the men were distracted, now was their chance.

Jesse turned to Sadie. "They're at the other end of the circle drive. This might be our best chance to run for the truck."

"Wait." She grabbed his arm, then pointed to his truck. "Look. Remember the gunshots earlier?"

He followed the line of her gaze, dread filling his stomach. All four tires were flat.

FOUR

A sickening sense of inadequacy threatened to consume him like a sinkhole. Long ago, Dale Madsen had told him he'd never be good enough for Sadie, reinforcing everything his uncle had drilled into his head for years. He'd proved her father right then, and he was proving him right again now.

"We have to take mine." Sadie's words snapped him out of his dark thoughts.

Now wasn't the time to wallow in regret; he could do that later, when they were safe.

Her lips pressed together as she nodded toward the closed garage door. "But my keys are inside the house." She glanced around the front again, then pointed back the way they'd come. "This way, follow me."

He jogged lightly after her as she ran past the three closed garage doors to a fourth standard door. Then she slid her fingers along the stonework near the foundation and came up with a key tucked somewhere in a crevice. A moment later, she had the door unlocked, and they slipped into the dark garage.

An old Ford pickup truck took up one of the spaces, but the other two held a snowblower, a riding lawnmower and an assortment of tools. He followed Sadie, dodging around a drill press and saw table until they reached a door leading into the house. She pushed it open a few inches, listening intently, then turned back to him.

"Nothing. They're still outside. I'll get the keys. You get Kip. Meet at the truck. Got it?"

He nodded, then followed her inside. As Sadie vanished toward the front, he whistled softly. "Kip? Where are you, boy?"

An answering whine came from a nearby closet, followed by a scratching sound. Relief filled his chest. Here was one thing he could do for Sadie, at least. He jogged over to the door and pulled it open, revealing the large collie crammed beneath a rack of coats. His tail wagged as he burst out, sniffing Jesse's hands. As he picked up the dog, Sadie came rushing back with a key ring in her hand.

"Come on," she urged, her face crimping like she was in pain. "You're driving."

"What's wrong?" Other than the obvious—those men outside. "Are you okay?"

"My head is killing me." She massaged her temple with her free hand.

He should've insisted she sleep earlier. "I'm sorry."

"I'll survive." She held the door open as he carried Kip into the garage. Sadie pointed toward the passenger door. "He'll have to sit on the bench between us. My truck doesn't have a back seat."

After he settled the dog inside, Sadie tossed him the keys and climbed in, leaving her door open. Jesse dashed around to the driver side, got in and stuck the keys in the ignition.

"They're going to hear it when we start the truck," he warned.

"Plus the garage door." Sadie pointed at the remote

clipped to the visor over his head. "You've got to open that, too."

"Take this, just in case." He held out the handgun he'd taken from Barts, and her dark eyes met his gaze. Sadie had lived her entire life on a ranch. She was a better shot than half the rangers he knew. "Ready?"

Her throat bobbed, but she nodded.

Lord, please protect us.

He punched the button for the garage door and switched on the ignition as Sadie slammed her door shut. As soon as the garage door opened enough to allow clearance for the vehicle, he threw the truck into Drive and whipped out of the garage. Kip tumbled toward Sadie, and she wrapped an arm around him. Gravel flew from beneath the tires as they hit the unpaved circle and barreled past his truck.

Shouting came from behind them, followed by loud gunshots that pinged off the tailgate.

"Keep your head down!" Jesse urged as he turned off the driveway loop and onto the dirt road, heading for the ranch entrance. The back end of the truck fishtailed as the tires fought for purchase on the loose gravel. In the rearview mirror, he could see the two men scrambling into their SUV. He punched the accelerator, urging the truck faster as they barreled toward the entrance of the ranch.

"They're coming!" Sadie yelled, her head craned over her shoulder.

They were approaching the county road fast. He scanned both directions, offering a silent prayer of thanks that the road was clear. "Hang on," he said, cranking the wheel to the left while hitting the accelerator. As soon as the front tires hit asphalt, the truck lurched forward, back tires squealing.

He glanced in the side mirror. The other vehicle was in hot pursuit, swerving out onto the main road behind them. When something flashed in the early morning light on the SUV's passenger side, he called, "Sadie, down!"

More bullets pinged off the tailgate. Sadie hunkered down in the seat, her arms wrapped around Kip, face pressed against his fur. She still held the gun in one hand, and she waved it as if in question when Jesse's eyes locked with hers.

"No." He shook his head. "Too dangerous when they're—"

With a sharp crack that made him jump, a bullet embedded in the rear glass between them. Fractures spider-webbed across the glass, threatening to break it at any moment. That was *way* too close. Sadie's eyes went wide.

He jerked the steering wheel to the left, swerving the truck across the double yellow line, then back as they approached a bend in the road. Anything to make them a harder target to hit. Where was the deputy?

The road curved to the right, and he was forced to tap the brakes as the truck lurched dangerously to the left. Kip slid across the seat. Flipping them certainly wouldn't help the situation.

But the other driver didn't share Jesse's concerns—the SUV zoomed forward, so close it nearly kissed the truck's rear bumper. Jesse punched the accelerator, trying to gain distance as the road straightened out, but Sadie's old truck didn't have the same power as the newer vehicle.

The blue hood filled his vision in the rearview mirror, so close he could see the nasty snarl on the other driver's face. "Hold on!" he yelled again, his fingers tightening around the steering wheel.

A jolting impact sent them lurching forward, and Kip's

hindquarters slid off the seat as Sadie fought to hold him close. Jesse clenched his jaw. If they crashed, Kip would go flying. But what could he do? There was nowhere to pull off, nowhere to hide in this open valley.

Sadie glanced behind them, then yelped as she wrapped herself over Kip. He felt the impact a fraction of a second later, this time accompanied by the horrible screeching sound of twisting metal. The steering wheel started to slide out of his grasp, and panic lanced through his system as he tightened his grip. But the front tires had already swerved to the right, hitting the rumble strips on the narrow shoulder and making his teeth clatter.

He fought to get the truck back on the road, but the other vehicle must've locked onto their bumper because it was like steering a seventy-ton military tank. A prayer shot through his mind like a breath as the front tires hit grass, bouncing and shaking the entire vehicle like it might fall apart—or flip—any minute. As much as he wanted to hit the brakes, he let the tires roll, wrestling with the steering wheel to keep them going as straight as he could.

In seconds it was over. The truck rolled to a stop, Kip and Sadie still intact in the seat next to him. Sweat coated his forehead, the back of his neck, his palms. Kip whined, and Sadie whispered softly to him.

Then a car door slammed shut right behind them. Sadie's gaze flew to Jesse's, her eyes wide. They both turned to see out the back. The two men stalked toward her truck, each carrying a gun.

They had seconds, at best, to get away before the men would have them at point-blank range. Jesse jerked back around, his foot slamming the gas at the same moment. The engine roared to life, and the tires spun as the truck strained to separate from the SUV locked onto its bumper. Metal creaked. If they could just break free...

Outside, one of the men yelled something, and a gunshot split the air, followed by secondary sharp bangs.

The truck listed forward, its tires instantly deflating. Another shot shattered the already damaged rear window, showering glass onto Jesse's neck and shoulders and across Sadie's back as she hunched over Kip.

His stomach plunged into his knees. They were trapped.

Sadie only had time to push Kip onto the floor and wrap both hands around the gun before the men were at the doors. One on each side, semiautomatic handguns aiming through the windows at their heads.

"Whatever happens, don't give up that gun," Jesse said, his tone edged with steel.

Her palms grew slick with sweat. Sure, she could shoot a can off a fence post a hundred yards away with a rifle, but she'd never shot at a person. Ever. The mere idea went against everything ingrained in her since childhood. Not to mention these men had the advantage.

"Out of the vehicle," the muscular man outside her window ordered. Sweat beaded on his thick forehead above blond eyebrows. "Both of you. And don't try nothin', or you won't live to see tomorrow."

He was far enough back he hadn't seen the gun in her hands. Should she raise it? Aim it at him? But then Jesse would be completely exposed. She should've made him take it—he was the one with law enforcement training.

"Jesse..." she murmured. *What do I do?*

"Now!" The man angled the barrel of the gun upward

and fired, shattering the glass of her passenger door and lodging a bullet in the roof of the cab.

Her heart jammed in her throat, and Kip barked loudly.

"Shut that dog up!" the man ordered, swiveling the gun back to her.

"Kip, quiet," Sadie commanded. Her voice shook. The gun in her hands shook. Every cell in her body shook.

"Do what he says, Sadie," Jesse said softly.

She wasn't sure she liked the dangerous gleam in his eye. Like he was going to try something reckless to save her. Maybe he'd broken her heart once, but that didn't mean he deserved to die helping her. She kept the gun tucked low against her leg as she reached for the door handle.

"Nice and slow," the man said, taking a step back from the truck.

Sadie sucked in a breath, then pulled the plastic handle. But as she eased the door open a few inches, Jesse flew into motion beside her, kicking his door open and into his attacker's outstretched gun. A shot went off, ricocheting off the hood. The man howled in pain, and Jesse leaped from the vehicle.

Before she could see what happened, the man closest to her flung her door open. As the handle slipped from her grasp, she placed both hands on the gun and raised it until they were facing off at point-blank range.

Grunts and thuds sounded from the other side of the truck, as if Jesse and the tall, lanky man were engaged in a fist fight. *Please protect him, Lord.*

Kip growled, nosing her leg. Pleading her to release him from the order to stay. "No, Kip, you stay," she ordered, her voice stronger now even though every nerve was on edge.

She may not know how to save her or Jesse's lives, but she could start with protecting Kip.

"Put the gun down and get out, little lady. Or it'll be your last mistake." The man kept his gun even, but his gaze kept darting over her shoulder to the chaos on the other side of the vehicle. If she could just buy more time, maybe Jesse would come out on top.

She swallowed. "Who hired you? What do you want with me?"

"My employer ain't none of your business. What is your business is doing what I say."

A shot fired behind her, and she winced as the man slowly smiled. The sounds of fighting had died away, but she didn't dare turn around to look. *Please, Lord, not Jesse.* He *had* to be all right. She couldn't live with his death on her hands, not when he had nothing to do with this mess.

Then another sound broke through their silent stalemate— a car engine heading their direction.

The man on the other side of the truck swore, and a police siren blared across the grassy meadow. "Davis, we gotta go. Now!" he yelled.

The man in front of her scowled, small eyes disappearing in his face, then he flicked his gaze toward the road and back to her. For one brief moment he stared at her, as if debating whether to shoot her. Then he began to back away, one step at a time. When he reached the SUV, he flung the passenger door open and dived inside.

The other man climbed into the driver seat, fired up the engine and threw the vehicle into Reverse.

Her truck shuddered from the sudden motion. Then, with a creaking split of metal, the truck's bumper tore loose and the SUV was free. The driver veered toward the road, dragging the bumper until it finally dropped off as the SUV bounced back onto the road.

She lowered her gun, arms trembling, and stared after it for a long moment until the sound of the approaching siren snapped her back to reality.

Jesse. Was he okay? She jumped out of the cab, then glanced back at Kip. "Release. Good boy."

The dog stood, nuzzling Sadie's hand, and she helped him jump out of the cab. When he dashed around the front of the truck, she followed, scanning the ground for Jesse. Her knees nearly gave way when she saw him push himself up into a sitting position.

Fifty yards away, the police cruiser pulled to a stop on the side of the road.

Jesse massaged a shoulder, then glanced between her and the disappearing SUV. "Thank the Lord, you're alive. I'm sorry, I couldn't stop—" He clamped his mouth shut. A muscle worked in his jaw, and in the bright morning light it almost looked like his eyes went glassy.

She knelt beside him, scanning him for any visible signs of injury. "I heard the gun fire. Did you get hit?"

"No. It missed," he said. From the bumps and bruises swelling on his face, he'd taken his fair share of hits. "What about you? Are you hurt?"

Her head throbbed like a gong repeatedly struck by a mallet. But no…she wasn't physically hurt. She shook her head, then took a moment to check Kip for injuries. Satisfied the dog wasn't hurt, she glanced up to see a police officer dashing across the field toward them.

"Ranger Taylor, Ms. Madsen," the officer said, crouching down beside them. Had she met him before? "Are you all right?"

Jesse shook his hand. "Deputy Griggs, excellent timing." He turned to Sadie. "Deputy Griggs was at your ranch last night. He's partnering with Deputy Freeman from the hospital on this case."

"Nice to meet you," she said, shaking his hand.

Together they helped Jesse to his feet, then she and Jesse explained to Deputy Griggs what had happened. The officer frowned as he listened, the crease between his brows deepening as they spoke. When they finished, he clicked on his shoulder radio and called in a report.

"Every officer in the Hole will be on the lookout for that SUV," he said, "and the sheriff's office has another deputy on the way to arrest the suspect in your pole barn. We'll get a tow truck out here, but if you're comfortable leaving the truck, I'll give you a ride back to the ranch."

"I'm fine with that," Sadie said. It wasn't like anyone could steal it in this condition. "Just let me grab a few things out of the glove box." While they waited, she retrieved her insurance card and other personal information, then called for Kip and walked with the others back to the squad car.

They arrived back at the ranch a short time later. Jesse's truck, with its four flat tires, sat forlornly between the house and the burnt skeleton of the horse stable. Her heart twisted as she surveyed the damage. Last night had been bad enough, but now she feared this was only the beginning.

"I need to secure the suspect in the barn," Deputy Griggs said as they pulled to a stop in front of the house. "If you'll wait inside, I'd like to go over the details again once he's in the back of the squad car."

Sadie stuffed her hands into her pockets to keep them from shaking, then led the way to the house. The adrenaline coursing through her veins for the last hour had ebbed away during the ride back, and now she felt empty and fragile inside, like a shell that might crack at the slightest touch. And the last thing she wanted was to fall apart in front of Jesse.

She was grateful for his help—she wouldn't have survived without him—but that didn't mean she wanted to turn into a vulnerable mess in front of him. No, she needed something to do, something to focus on besides her own fragility. Like those swelling lumps on his face. And hot coffee to fortify her crumbling insides.

"You sit," she told Jesse after letting them inside the front door. "I'll get you some ice for that face. You're swelling up like you approached the wrong end of a bucking bronco."

"Yes, ma'am." A smile cracked his lips. Somehow, despite the growing bruises, he managed to look just as handsome as ever. Maybe even more so, since he'd earned all those welts helping her.

She shook away the unsettling thoughts as he plopped onto the couch. Kip jumped up next to him, curling his furry body right up next to Jesse's leg like they were best friends.

Just great. Even her dog loved him. Sadie blew a strand of hair out of her face as she went into the kitchen and started up the coffeepot. Kip didn't know the whole story, or he wouldn't be so cozy with the man who'd taken her heart and trampled it like a mustang thrashing a rattlesnake. He'd left her to handle the disastrous aftermath all alone. She'd had to cancel the contracts with the wedding vendors, notify all the guests—the humiliation still scorched the back of her neck—*and* deal with their bickering families. Her father had stayed tight-lipped about Jesse's abrupt departure, but Rob Clark had lost no time in blaming Dale and Sadie. As if any of it had been *her* fault.

She shook off the horrible memories as she wrapped up a bag of ice in a kitchen towel. Then she grabbed a clean mug, poured coffee and added cream and sugar. After giving the ice pack and mug to Jesse, she returned to get her own coffee.

For a moment, she leaned against the kitchen island, letting the steaming liquid scald her throat on the way down. The burn felt good. Reassuring. Something familiar when everything else had come untethered. Words from her Bible came into her mind. *The Lord is my rock and my fortress and my deliverer.* Jesus was her firm foundation, the One she was supposed to be finding strength in.

Not coffee.

Her lips curved as she laughed at herself. *Help me to stand strong in You, Lord*, she prayed. The Lord would get her through this, the same way He'd gotten her through her failed engagement and her parents' deaths. He'd sent Jesse to help her right when she needed it, but now that the police deputy was here, she would manage.

Jesse might not like it, but it was time for him to go.

Jesse pressed the cold pack against his face, imagining for a moment that he was one of those cartoon characters holding a big slab of raw steak against his cheek. He felt like *he* was raw meat, after all the punches Warden had managed to land.

Things could have gone much worse, though, and he offered a silent prayer of thanks that they'd escaped with their lives.

He glanced up as Sadie came back into the room, carrying a coffee cup in front of her like a shield. She sat in a chair near the opposite end of the sofa, like she wanted as much space from him as possible. Clearly, she still didn't trust him. Or forgive him. Not that he blamed her. No, he understood her feelings more than she realized.

Another apology sprang to his lips, or maybe just an explanation. *Let me tell you why I left.* But then he clamped his mouth shut. Telling her what her father had said to him wouldn't undo the past, and it would only tarnish her memories of Dale. Let the blame fall squarely on Jesse, because no matter what anyone had said to him, ultimately *he* was the one who had decided to pack up and leave. Nobody put a gun to his head and made him do it.

Dale's words had hurt him—no doubt about that—but Dale hadn't physically forced him out. Instead, he'd merely confirmed what Uncle Rob had been telling Jesse all along, that he wasn't worthy of Sadie's love. The funny thing was, even though Dale and Rob's friendship had ruptured months prior, Dale had still been kind to Jesse up until the end. Almost like the father he no longer had. He'd never understood what changed Dale's mind. All he knew was that he'd absorbed each painful word and seen no alternative but to cut ties and run. Straight into the National Park Service, where nature wouldn't tell him he was a disappointment, and the squirrels didn't care whether his shoes had been shined.

A knock at the door roused him from the painful memories. Sadie set her mug down on the coffee table and went to the door, then returned with Deputy Griggs. He took a seat in the chair opposite Sadie, then glanced between her and Jesse.

"The man you tied up in the barn—Barts?" They nodded, and he went on, "He was gone. He must've come to and managed to escape on foot."

The hairs stood up on the back of Jesse's neck. He glanced around the house, then back to Sadie. Her knuckles whitened on her mug.

"Could he still be on my property, then?" she asked.

The deputy frowned. "That's a possibility, though not likely. I suspect he'd want to get away before he got caught, considering he's on foot."

"Unless he stole one of my horses." One of Sadie's hands balled into a fist. "I still haven't recovered all of them after last night."

We'll find them, Jesse wanted to reassure her. But that wasn't guaranteed, and besides, there wouldn't be a *we* for much longer.

"There's another deputy on the way. We'll search the property thoroughly, ma'am. You don't need to worry about anyone else harming you."

Her eyes flitted to Jesse's, something flashing in their brown depths. Maybe, *Get lost. You can go now*? He leaned back on the sofa, settling in against the cushions. He wasn't going anywhere, not until Zeke and Lottie arrived and he could be absolutely sure she wasn't in danger.

From the way her lips thinned, she got the message.

Oblivious to their secret conversation, the deputy said, "I'd like to go over a few things while we're waiting for Deputy Willis." When Sadie nodded, he went on. "You told Deputy Freeman last night about the offers you've had on the ranch."

"Oh, here," Jesse said, digging into his pocket. He handed the deputy the note they'd found under Sadie's door. "We found it this morning in the entryway, right after they tried to run us off the road the first time."

Deputy Griggs took the paper and scanned it briefly, then tucked it into an evidence bag. "You told my partner that your ranch is held in a trust, and that the attacks have been escalating ever since the geologist you hired found oil. Does the trust include both the mineral and surface rights?"

She nodded. "Yes, the ranch is a unified estate. All the rights are held in a legacy trust my grandfather put together."

"And you have no children, correct?" the deputy asked.

"That's correct." Her gaze flicked to Jesse, so quickly he almost missed it.

For a second, a different life flashed before his eyes. What would have happened if he'd stayed? Would he and Sadie have two or three chubby-cheeked little ones running around? The oldest might be big enough to sit a pony by now. Something burned inside his chest, painful and raw, but he shoved it away.

That wasn't how things had turned out, and he'd have to trust the Lord that it was better this way. He couldn't undo any of the choices that younger Jesse had made.

Sadie continued after a nearly imperceptible pause. "I'm the last living beneficiary."

A sinking feeling doused the burning in Jesse's chest, as he realized where the deputy was going with this. Who would benefit from Sadie's death? "Who takes over the trust if something happens to you?"

"My dad designated some charity years ago."

"Do you know the name of it, Ms. Madsen?" the deputy asked. He'd pulled out a notepad and pen.

She shook her head. "I'm not sure Dad ever told me which one he picked. I'd have to check with Mike Schmidt at Jackson Financial. He's the designated financial advisor who was assigned as trustee. Actually, he's a cotrustee with me. But it makes this whole situation even more ridiculous. I couldn't even sell to these people if I wanted to, without Jackson Financial signing off on the deal."

Jesse leaned forward, propping his elbows up on his knees. "Sadie, does the charity know they're named as beneficiary? Is there a chance someone there might be after you?"

"I don't know if Dad ever told them." She massaged her temples. "I certainly haven't. But I guess anything is possible. I need to schedule a meeting with Mike anyway to talk about the insurance after the fire and to review the trust's financial status. I can ask him tomorrow about the charity."

Deputy Griggs frowned. "Please do. We should follow every available lead. In the meantime, we'll process the evidence we've collected and continue searching for these men. I'll also follow up on Senator Fitz and your neighbor, Mr. Johnson."

Sadie's phone rang. While she answered, Jesse leaned closer to the deputy. "I'm concerned about her safety. Can the sheriff's office send a cruiser out here to keep watch?"

"That's a good idea," Griggs said, nodding. "I'll call in the request. Deputy Willis can take the first shift, since he won't need to bring in the man who escaped."

At the other end of the sofa, Sadie clicked off the call. "That was the towing company. They're hauling the truck into town for me. I asked them to send someone out to take care of your tires," she told Jesse. "That way you won't be stuck here."

From the stone set of her features and the way she avoided meeting his gaze, she was counting down the minutes until his departure.

He stood. Might as well be helpful before he left. "Guess I'll get back to work on those horses as long as I'm here. And let me give you my cell number, just in case anything comes up." Despite the edge to her expression, she dutifully entered the number as he read it off. It only made sense, after everything they'd been through, to swap contact information.

Deputy Griggs rose also, and Sadie led the way to the door.

"I'll be out front collecting evidence from last night's fire," he said, "if you need anything."

"Thank you," Sadie said, opening the door for him.

Jesse followed him out, then held up a hand when Sadie tried to follow. "I know your head still hurts. You need to take some ibuprofen and rest. I know where to find you if anything comes up that requires your help."

He expected her to argue, saw the way her lips parted, so he placed both hands on her shoulders and gently turned her around. A whiff of mint and lavender filled his nose, but he ignored the intoxicating, specifically Sadie scent and jabbed a finger toward the back hall. "That way, Sadie. Don't show your face unless there's an emergency, got it? And in that case, just text me instead of getting out of bed."

She took a few hesitant paces, then stopped and looked back at him.

He held two fingers up, pointing to his own eyes, then her face, as if to say, *I'm watching you.*

Her mouth hitched on one side, rewarding him with an almost-smile, but then the weariness settled back over her small frame, and she turned away, vanishing down the hall.

Jesse sighed. Having that woman back in his life, however temporarily, was far more difficult than he'd imagined. The past was over and done with, and yet…he couldn't shake the feeling he'd made the wrong choice all those years ago. It had nearly crushed him at the time, but he'd gotten over her. Or so he'd thought. But being this close to her again, imagining what could've been...

It hurt. So bad his breath snagged in his chest when he let himself think about the regret. The guilt.

Which meant he needed to *not* think about her in that way anymore and instead focus on doing what needed to be done. Otherwise, he'd just be opening himself up to the possibility of going through all that pain again, and that was out of the question.

FIVE

Sadie awoke swaddled in a cozy blanket, the delicious sense of comfort dragging her achy limbs deeper into the soft bed. The feeling only lasted for a second before reality came crashing back in—the fire, the blue SUV, the police, Jesse. She rubbed bleary eyes, glancing at the clock, then groaned. It was early afternoon. She should've told Jesse to wake her sooner.

She forced herself up, swinging her legs over the side of the bed. At least the pounding in her head had subsided to a dull pain that she could almost pretend wasn't there. But the rest of it… There was no pretending all these disasters away.

Sighing, she picked up her cell and scrolled through her notifications. Three texts from Katrina about getting coffee next week. She couldn't put off her friend forever, so she tapped out a quick message.

The horse stable caught on fire last night. I'm fine, just have a lot to deal with. Will explain later. Also guess who showed up? Jesse Taylor.

She'd barely managed to pull up Mike Schmidt's number at Jackson Financial before her friend shot back a reply.

Your ex-fiancé? Spill the details asap.

A smile curved her lips, but Katrina would have to wait. Can't now, but don't worry, you'll hear it all later.

She tapped back over to Mike's number and clicked the Call button. She'd only met with him a couple of times— once after her parents' accident, so he could explain the basics of the trust, and then again last year when the ranch's finances had started to tank, and she wanted to explore their options. He'd been opposed to selling at the time, and she fully expected him to side with her now. Though with another insurance claim to make, she could use his advice on the best way to proceed.

Mike's personal line rang four times before her call was bumped back to an office assistant, who scheduled a meeting for her the following afternoon. She clicked off the call and dragged her sore body out of bed, then took a few minutes to rebraid her hair and straighten her appearance. Maybe if she could get through all the day's tasks, she'd be able to squeeze in a ride before night fell. Getting out on horseback, away from life's demands and Jesse's presence, sounded like heaven right now.

But first she had to deal with him.

Some of the knots in her stomach loosened when she went out front and found a repair truck parked next to his Dodge Ram. All four tires had been replaced, and the driver was shaking Jesse's hand. A pair of police cruisers sat parked on the other side of the circle drive. And better yet, from that cloud of dust hovering on the horizon near the entrance to her ranch, the Nelsons were here. She drew in a deep breath of fresh mountain air, letting the warm afternoon sunshine kiss her skin. Things were definitely looking up.

As soon as the repairman climbed into his truck, Sadie headed over to where Jesse was inspecting his new tires.

"Looks like you're all set," she said. At her voice, Kip came dashing around the truck and nuzzled her with his nose. She scratched him behind the ears and tried not to notice how attractive Jesse looked in his blue jeans and T-shirt.

Jesse stood, his sharp gaze running from her toes up to her face. "Did you get some rest? You look better." He froze, then held up his hand. "Not that you didn't look good before. I mean, you've always been—" At her expression, he cut off. "Never mind."

"Yes, I got some rest," she said, letting her scowl soften. They'd been through a lot today, and he'd been nothing but helpful and concerned. "My head's feeling much better. Maybe now that you know I'm not at death's door, you can feel free to go home."

"I found the other horses." He leaned back against the truck, crossing his arms over his chest. His flannel shirt was gone, and his tanned biceps were clearly visible beneath his short sleeves. She toed the dirt, then turned toward the pole barn despite the fact she wasn't going to see the horses from here. "Even the big black stud. Orion, you said?"

"Yeah. Did he cooperate with you?"

Jesse shrugged. "I showed him who was boss."

At the gleam in his eyes, her lips cracked despite herself. "You mean Kip?"

Her dog barked, and Jesse laughed. "Righto. Kip found him and got him back to the barn. All I did was hold the stall door open."

"Good boy," she said, scratching the collie behind the ears. He stood, tail wagging, and abandoned her to nudge Jesse's leg. She tucked her chin to her chest. Why did everyone have to like that man so much? Even her traitorous animals? Although he'd given Kip the credit, truth was, even Zeke had a hard time getting Orion to cooperate. And yet Jesse could waltz in here after all these years, and they all loved him.

Relief pulsed through her as the Nelsons' truck pulled up behind Jesse's. Finally, he could go, before she felt tempted to forgive him. "Zeke and Lottie are back."

The couple, in their late fifties, climbed out of the vehicle. Lottie swept Sadie into a lemon-scented hug as Zeke shook hands with Jesse. For an awful moment Sadie was struck with how *normal* it all felt, like this was the way things were supposed to be. Her throat closed on an unexpected swell of longing. She cleared it, then crossed her arms.

Why had Jesse made sure this wasn't their life? She *knew* he'd loved her. Even that awful day when he left, she'd known—with a conviction so deep she could feel it in the marrow of her bones.

So why had he walked away?

With the way his uncle and her father had been at each other in the months leading up to his abrupt departure, she felt certain there was more to the story. She and Jesse had both tried to get out of them what had happened, but other than occasional insinuations about the other's poor judgement or bad character, they'd never gotten a conclusive answer. In the end, they'd figured maybe a business deal had gone sour.

Despite the family tension, everything had seemed fine

between her and Jesse until that moment he turned up in the barn and dumped her.

Eventually she'd known it was time to let him go his own stubborn way. He could live his life regretting what he'd given up, and she'd forget about him and make her dreams for the ranch come true. It was his own fault.

Anger fired up in her gut again, and after waiting patiently for a few minutes while he caught Zeke up on the situation, she turned to him. "Thanks for everything, Jesse, but we don't want to keep you any longer." She pointed toward the Teton Range across the valley. "You've got a whole national park to protect, not just my ranch."

He'd been petting Kip, but at her words, his gaze pivoted to her with breath-stopping focus. For a second the rest of the world vanished, and there was only the endless glacial blue of his eyes, staring at her with an intensity that could bore through her soul. "Protecting you is far more important."

Something about the way he said it, in a low rumble meant only for her, stopped her lungs from working correctly. So when he stuck out his hand to shake, she took it. The feel of his palm against hers, warm and rough and strong, brought back a thousand memories in a single touch, so sharp and fast she jerked her hand back as if he'd burned it.

She tucked both hands into her pockets and cleared her throat. "Thank you again for your help. I'm sure one of the deputies will be in touch if they need anything from you."

His gaze lingered a fraction longer, then he nodded once, his chin set. "See you, Sadie. Stay safe."

The words carried an air of finality, and she hated the way something twisted inside her chest, as if *she* was the one running *him* off.

Well, that wasn't how it had happened the first time, was it? She could hardly be blamed for not trusting him or wanting his help now. Besides, she had a ranch to save, and the last thing she needed was a handsome ex-fiancé distracting her. She'd gotten along just fine without him all these years.

He waved to Zeke and Lottie and climbed into his truck, then took off without looking back. The painful thing in her chest deflated, and she sighed wearily. Why did everything have to be so hard? *Lord, I just need a break.* When Lottie pulled her into another hug, she melted into the older woman's arms.

"Why don't you come inside and let me fix you a cup of coffee?" Lottie asked.

Sadie swiped at her eyes before any telltale tears sprang loose and shook her head. "I've got to assess the damage and call the insurance company. I haven't had time to yet." She turned to Zeke. Like his wife, his hair had grayed over the years, and he'd developed creases in his forehead and around his mouth, but he'd only grown more capable in managing the ranch. Sadie didn't know what she'd do without him. "Jesse moved the horses to the pole barn."

"I'll check on them first, then see what we've got left." He tipped his head toward the blackened ribs of the horse stable, where one of the deputies could be seen taking pictures with a camera. Then Zeke's gaze connected with his wife's, who nodded slightly. "Lottie and I think it would be best if we stayed with you in the house, if you don't object."

Sadie drew in a shuddering breath, grateful they'd offered. "Thank you, I'd appreciate that, given the circumstances."

That was the one downside to sending Jesse away—as

much as she hated to admit it, he'd done everything in his power to keep her alive. In fact, if she were being honest, she felt safe with him, safer than she had in long time.

She tried to shake away the unsettling thoughts over the afternoon as she picked through the remains of her barn with the deputy and Zeke. They cataloged what had been lost and took pictures and salvaged a couple of things she might be able to clean. Any hopes of an evening ride vanished as she sat on the phone with the insurance company for an eternity. By the time she'd eaten a warm bowl of Lottie's delicious chili, it was all she could do to crawl back to her room and collapse into bed.

The next morning, when sunlight streaked in between her curtains and slanted warm across her face, the same dismal sense of oppression lay heavy on her spirit. She shuddered, then her gaze fell on the small, framed calligraphy Bible verse her grandmother had given her when she was only a little girl.

It is of the Lord's mercies that we are not consumed, because His compassions fail not. They are new every morning: great is Thy faithfulness.

The words sang to her, beckoning her to sink into them and find peace in God's presence. But how could she, after what had happened to her barn—to her life? Maybe once everything had settled down and was back under control, she'd be able to rest in God's promises. Until then, she needed to take action. And she'd already overslept.

She sprang out of bed and hauled on a clean pair of jeans and a button-down shirt, then padded out to the kitchen.

"Morning, sweetheart," Lottie said cheerfully. The older

woman handed her a steaming mug of coffee and a plate of sizzling bacon and scrambled eggs. "Zeke's already out with the horses. We're both glad you got some sleep."

Guilt racked Sadie's insides. Lottie shouldn't be cooking for her, and Zeke had enough on his plate without doing all Sadie's jobs, too. "Thank you," she said. "You don't have to keep cooking for me, though. I hate for you to have this extra work."

"Now, you don't worry about us," she said, wiping the countertop with a dishcloth. "You've got enough to deal with already. How are you feeling today?"

Sadie took her food to the kitchen island and sat on one of the stools at the counter. Her body still felt stiff and achy, but her head had improved significantly. "Sore but better, I think." If only there were something she could do about her heart and the painful places inside that Jesse's reappearance had stirred up.

As she ate, her phone buzzed with an incoming text. "Good news, my truck should be ready this afternoon."

Lottie looked up from the kitchen sink. "Perfect, let me give you a ride into town. I need to stop by the store anyway."

Hours later, she climbed into her truck at the repair shop near the small airport. Now for this meeting with Mike. Hopefully they could come up with a plan to start rebuilding once the investigation ended.

Deputy Griggs had finished his work at the barn and taken the evidence back for analysis, leaving another officer patrolling her property. They hadn't found the blue SUV or caught the men yet, but hopefully it was only a matter of time. Now that the authorities were involved, surely whoever was behind this would give up.

She pulled out of the repair place and steered onto the highway leading into town. Her meeting with Mike was scheduled in twenty-five minutes, giving her just enough time to get there, park and mentally prepare. If the insurance company came through with money to replace the stable, she could almost get back on track. But she wanted to talk to him about the oil. As much as she hated the idea of a rig on her property, maybe leasing the mineral rights could give her enough extra cash to begin renovating the main house for guests.

The possibilities sparked something in her chest, a sense of hope she hadn't felt in a long time. Maybe, just maybe, God would bring something good out of this awful mess.

But when she glanced into her rearview mirror, the good feelings evaporated like water on a hot summer day. A very familiar-looking blue Ford Explorer had pulled out of a parking lot on the opposite side of the highway. Almost as if they'd been waiting for her to leave the repair shop. The hairs on her neck stood up at the thought of being watched. She might have a chance at losing them in town, but she still had miles to go before she'd reach the city limits.

She glanced both ways up and down the highway. Traffic was light, but that would change the closer she got to town. Maybe she could lead them north to Teton. The front gate would be crawling with park rangers, and if she could notify Jesse in advance...

Sadie waited until a side road opened on the left and swerved the truck into a sudden U-turn, using the extra pavement to keep her vehicle on asphalt. Not expecting the move, the driver of the SUV flew past, but then swung the vehicle into a turn in the middle of the road up ahead, his tires hitting gravel and grass on the side of the two-lane road. An approaching car honked as they narrowly avoided a collision.

She slammed her foot on the gas and fumbled in the center console for her phone, then initiated the voice command. "Call Jesse Taylor." His phone rang. "Please pick up, please pick up..." she muttered, grateful she had his contact information.

"Sadie?" he answered. Even through her tinny phone speaker, she could hear the worry in his voice. "What's up?"

She tightened her grip on the wheel, banking the truck around a curve. "I've got some old friends on my tail." He groaned at her words, but she kept going. "Heading up 191 toward Moose. Can you notify the rangers at the gate?"

"Did you call the cops yet?"

"Not yet. I'm closer to you." Why did she feel the need to explain? Especially with that SUV gaining on her? She pushed the truck faster, thankful that the brand-new tires gripped the road far better than her old set had.

"Hang tight, Sadie. You can do this. Stay on the line with me."

His words gave a little extra strength to her spine as she clutched the steering wheel. In the background she could hear him talking, though the words weren't distinguishable. No doubt calling for help on his radio or another phone line. As much as she hated to admit it, the idea of contacting him for help instead of the police had brought an extra measure of reassurance, because she *knew* he would do anything to help her.

The Explorer pulled dangerously close, and she floored the accelerator. *Come on*, she urged the old truck, watching the speedometer creep higher and higher. Way *too* high to be safe on this twisty road.

She rounded a bend, and panic tugged at her already taut nerves as the big brown Grand Teton National Park entrance sign came into view on the right.

Up ahead, a red truck towing a pop-up camper was braking to pull into the turnout lined with RVs and other vehicles. Happy vacationers stood in front of the sign taking photographs, oblivious to the recklessly speeding truck and SUV heading their way.

If she hit the brakes, the Explorer would crash into her, but if she swerved, she'd have a head-on collision with the oncoming cars leaving the national park.

With no other alternative as she barreled toward the trailer, she lay on the horn, praying no one would pull out of the turnout in front of her. The red truck swerved onto the shoulder as it made the turn, and she narrowly avoided scraping the pop-up as she flew past. Another horn split the air, and in her rearview mirror she could see the driver of the red truck shaking his head at her.

It's not my fault! She gritted her teeth and concentrated on the road ahead. In a minute she'd need to take a ninety-degree left off this highway and onto the road that led to the park entrance at Moose. And then, if this reckless driver was foolish enough to follow, the authorities would get him.

She checked the rearview mirror. On this straight stretch, the SUV was gaining, even though she was pushing the truck as hard as she could. If she wasn't careful, she'd fly right past the turn and—

"Sadie?" Jesse's voice came through the phone again. "What was that? Are you all right?"

"Yeah, just about nailed a trailer turning off for a photo op at the sign."

"Then you're almost to me. You're going to take a sharp

left onto Teton Park Road in another minute or so. We're setting up a barricade across the Snake River. Once you get through it, take your first right into the lot for headquarters. I'll meet you there." The low rumble of his voice rolled around her, soothing and confident and calm, despite how every muscle in her body was taut as a bowstring.

"'Kay," she said, gulping when she glanced back at the SUV again. It was almost as if the driver sensed he was running out of real estate, and he'd redoubled his efforts to attack her newly replaced bumper.

Up ahead, she could see the pavement open to the left, with signs marking the turn into the Moose entrance. Her palms grew slick against the wheel. How was she going to brake for this turn without getting rammed? Or worse, losing control and flying into the river?

She gritted her teeth as the turn came closer. Closer. A few hundred yards away across the river, rangers scrambled with orange and white striped barricades. Would the other driver see it? Would it be enough to deter him?

At the last second, she cranked the wheel to the right and veered full speed onto the shoulder, then slammed the brakes. The truck shook so hard her bones rattled, but as she'd hoped, the pursuing vehicle went flying past. She punched the gas again and turned to the left, crossing over to Teton Park Road. Behind her on the highway, the blue SUV kept going. A moment later sirens blared in front of her, and a white-and-green National Park Service vehicle flew past her out onto the highway, giving chase.

She slowed to a snail's pace as she passed through the hastily assembled barricade, where a ranger waved her through. When she pulled into the headquarters lot and

saw Jesse waiting on the sidewalk outside the main building, a sob lodged in her throat, choking her with relief.

That had been way too close.

As soon as Sadie's white F-150 rolled to a stop, Jesse
dashed around to the driver door and flung it open. Sadie
turned dazed eyes up at him, then stumbled out of the seat
and into his open arms. He held her to his chest for a moment before releasing her, keeping his hand on her elbow
to help steady her. Adrenaline had to be gushing through
her already taxed system.

"It's okay. I'm here." He repeated the words until her
gaze cleared and met his.

"I almost hit someone. I couldn't get away from him."
Her whole body trembled like she'd been caught in a bliz-
zard without a coat. "How did they know where I was?"

"They must've followed you. You're safe now. I'm here."
He watched her closely for any signs of further injury.

She blinked up at him, her wide brown eyes liquid and
vulnerable, then they dropped to where his hand still supported her elbow. Reluctantly he pulled away. "I'm fine,
Jesse. Thank you for the help."

The openness vanished from her face, and he squared
his shoulders and moved a step back. She'd always been
independent—her fiery strength was one of the things
that had made him fall for her years ago—but for once he
wished she'd back off and slow down. Get some rest. Let
others shoulder the burdens for a bit.

"Come on in and let me get you a cup of coffee," he said,
throwing a thumb at park headquarters.

Instead of answering, she reached into her truck, fid-
dled around in the center console and came up with her

phone. He'd already ended their call as soon as her truck had pulled into the parking lot unscathed. But she swiped past the lock screen as if to double-check, then shook her head. "I'm going to be so late for my meeting with Mike." She tapped at her contacts without looking up. Faint ringing came from her phone, and she held it up to her ear, then glanced at him. "Do you think it's safe for me to head back to town, now that rangers are tailing those guys?"

Jesse sighed, soul deep. This woman needed some serious intervention. He propped one foot up on the driver running board to let her know she wasn't going anywhere. "No, Sadie, it's *not* safe. Did you not notice the vehicle that just tried to run you off the road for the third time in two days?" His chest grew hot. "Until those men are caught, you're not stirring out of my sight."

Her jaw worked, like she was preparing a comeback, but then a voice came on the other end of the line.

"Tell him you need to reschedule," he insisted. "Sometime when I can go with you. Or Zeke. Or a police officer. Or anyone who didn't experience a head injury two days ago."

She clamped her eyes shut, then reopened them and spoke into the phone. "Hi, Mike, I'm so sorry I won't make our meeting, but something came up. I'll call back to reschedule tomorrow." After clicking off, she shoved the phone into her pocket. "It went to voice mail. And since you're so insistent on me not going anywhere, I'll take you up on that cup of coffee."

As she stepped away from the truck, one leg wobbled. Jesse cupped his hand beneath her elbow again to stabilize her. She froze, and the small space between them crackled with memories and regrets sharper than static electricity.

Her chest rose and fell a few times as she took some deep breaths.

"You can let go," she said softly without looking at him. "I'm fine now. Just a little more rattled than I thought."

He released his grip but kept close to her as they walked inside, unease gnawing at his gut. There was no way he was letting Sadie leave his sight, not until those men were caught. Sure, technically she wasn't his responsibility, but he was in a better position to help her than just about anyone else.

"Have a seat, Sadie," he said, opening the door to a small conference room. They'd have more privacy here than in the big office space he shared with the other law enforcement rangers stationed at Moose. "I'll grab us some coffee."

When he returned a few minutes later, she had her elbows propped up on the table, massaging her forehead. He set the mug down in front of her. "Can I get you anything else? Water? Ibuprofen?"

She pulled her hands away from her temples and looked up at him, her skin red from rubbing. Seeing her like this—almost as broken as the day he'd walked out on her—made his chest ache. The last time all that pain had been *his* fault, but not now. Now, he could do something about it.

"No, thanks," she said. "Any update on the SUV?"

He shook his head. "Last I heard rangers were still in pursuit heading north. If you're feeling up to it, I'm going to call in the chief ranger and get Deputy Freeman on the phone. I figure it'll be easier if you only have to go over this once."

She drew in a long breath, then gave him a grateful smile. "Thanks."

Half an hour later, he and Chief Ranger Whit Morgan

sat at the table with Sadie. Deputies Freeman and Griggs had both been available and were listening through the speakerphone as Sadie relayed exactly what had happened. The fact the police hadn't managed to catch the SUV made anger spark in Jesse's stomach, but his own team of rangers hadn't done any better. While Sadie was sharing her story, an update had come through over his radio. The rangers had lost contact with the SUV somewhere between Moose and Moran, but with its license plate number identified, they'd find it as soon as it reappeared on the road.

There wasn't much out here in the way of civilization— they'd have to make a reappearance eventually—and in the meantime, the rangers hadn't given up searching the many unpaved side roads along the route. But Jesse wouldn't sleep well until those men were caught.

And they *still* had to figure out who had hired them.

"Did the analysis come back on any of the evidence from the ranch?" he asked the deputies once Sadie was done.

"Boot print by the creek was a size eleven, tread from Timberland brand," Griggs said.

Nothing helpful there... Half the men in the county wore those boots.

"The metal bar from Ms. Madsen's barn door only had Ranger Taylor's fingerprints, so it's likely the perpetrator wore gloves," Deputy Freeman said. "But we did get prints off the gun you recovered from the assailant in the pole barn. The prints match the gun's registry to one Justin Barts. He's a Natrona County resident."

"Casper area?" the chief ranger asked.

"Yes," Freeman confirmed, "so it's likely he's a hired hand for whoever is after Ms. Madsen. We're working on a warrant to pull his financial information to see if he's received any large payments recently, but so far we can't connect him to any of the names Ms. Madsen gave us."

"So, we still don't know who's after me?" Sadie asked.

"No, ma'am, not yet. But we did find evidence that the fire in your barn wasn't an accident. Based on the burn pattern, the fire started in the northeast corner of the barn near ground level. We found concentrated traces of kerosene residuals at the start point but no evidence of any kerosene storage."

She gave the phone a look. "I wouldn't have stored flammable chemicals in my horse stable, Deputy Freeman."

"Our thoughts exactly," he replied. "We'll get the report written up for your insurance company. In the meantime, we'll keep an officer stationed at your home, and I'd recommend you lie low for a few days. Stay home where our patrol can protect you."

"She's staying with me in the national park until we catch the suspects," Jesse said. When Sadie's surprised gaze flashed to his, he kept his expression stern. Now wasn't the time to argue. "Those men are still out there, and I'm going to make sure she stays safe."

She hugged her arms to her chest but, surprisingly, didn't object.

After the call ended, Jesse stepped out into the hall with the chief ranger.

"Do you want me to find a place for her to stay?" Whit asked.

Jesse shook his head. As awkward as it sounded having his ex-fiancée couch surf at his house, he wasn't about to let her out of his sight. "She'll be fine on my sofa."

Whit smiled gently. "I take it she's a close personal friend of yours?"

"You could say that." Jesse sighed. "We've got a little history, and I care about her. A lot. What matters most right now is keeping her safe."

The other man clapped him on the shoulder. "Then she's in good hands, Ranger Taylor. Let me know if you need any time off to handle this situation."

"Thanks." His new boss was a good man, and Jesse couldn't help offering up a silent prayer of gratitude as he returned to Sadie.

She stood as he entered, arms still wrapped across her stomach. "Are you sure about this? Because you don't have to take me in, I could just—"

"I'm sure." He leaned forward, propping his hands on the table. "My plan is to leave your truck here, where there are security cameras on the lot, and we'll walk to my place. Ranger housing is right behind this building. You can tag along with me on patrol tomorrow, unless we get word those men have been caught. The Nelsons can handle the ranch just fine for a couple of days. Deal?"

When she nodded, he extended his hand to make her shake on it. She hesitated a moment, then slid her hand into his. Electricity sparked up his arm at her touch, same as it had in the hospital a couple nights ago, and he had to resist the urge to pull back. From the way Sadie blushed, she felt it, too.

He stuffed his hands in his pockets as he led the way out the back door of the building. That intense connection he felt with her was just a physical reaction, a memory of what they'd once shared, nothing more.

After how badly he'd hurt her last time, she'd never give him another chance. Not that he'd ask for one, anyway. Opening up to her now would only put his heart at risk, if she rejected him the way her father had. And why wouldn't she, after what he'd done? He'd failed her, and he'd failed himself.

What mattered right now was keeping her safe, both from those men trying to hurt her and from the man who'd hurt her most of all—him. And that meant feelings for Sadie Madsen were out of the question.

Forever.

SIX

Sadie tossed and turned all night like she was on a bronco at the rodeo instead of a decently comfortable sectional sofa. The blue SUV haunted her dreams, sometimes spearing the side of her truck, other times chasing her horses or crashing through her front door.

Even more disconcerting was the number of times Jesse appeared in these nightmares, trying to help her escape, saving her at the last second. And at least once, he'd folded her against his chest, so close she could hear his heart beating. In her dream, she'd melted into the safety of his arms like she had yesterday after the car chase.

She awoke to the sound of dishes clinking in the nearby kitchen and a bittersweet sense of nostalgia and security. Once upon a time, she *had* fit neatly into his arms, but she had to remember those days were long gone. Just because he was helping her now didn't mean she could let down her guard. He'd broken her heart once, and she wasn't going to give him the chance to do it again. She couldn't. Besides, she had a ranch to save as soon as this mess was over.

"Hey," he called from the kitchen when she sat up. "Coffee's hot, and I've got some toast and eggs for you. How'd you sleep?"

"I, uh, fine," she mumbled. Better than the truth: *I dreamed about you*. She hadn't dreamed about him in years. That warm place beneath her ribs needed to chill out.

She glanced down at herself, frowning at her rumpled clothes and hair. Loose strands jutted out of her braid like improperly baled hay. Why was it, that after all these years, Jesse was only seeing her at her worst? *Doesn't matter*. "Let me just run to the bathroom."

She scurried over the cold linoleum floor and into the bathroom. He'd scrounged up an extra toothbrush and some other essentials for her, but she didn't like being here. Didn't like how the whole house carried his faint scent of leather and cedarwood, or how every single item made her think of him and the life they were supposed to have together.

All these feelings had burned out long ago, so why was she taking a stick and stirring up the cold ashes?

After brushing her teeth, she washed her face and tugged her hair out of its braid. The hair fell long and wavy halfway to her waist. If she left it down, loose and relaxed, would it help her insides loosen up, too? Judging by these dark half-moons under her eyes, and the ugly greenish bruise on her forehead, she needed all the relaxing she could get.

With a sigh, she flipped off the light and left her dissatisfying reflection behind. When she entered the kitchen, Jesse glanced at her, then did a double take, his gaze stalling on her hair. She tucked a strand behind her ear, suddenly self-conscious. Maybe she should've rebraided it.

"Here, take a seat," he said, springing forward to pull a chair out for her. He wore his NPS uniform—dark green pants and a taupe-colored shirt bearing the brown NPS arrowhead logo on the sleeve.

As she sat, she asked, "Any word on the driver of the

Explorer?" Last night they'd learned that the SUV had been found abandoned on a dirt road out past Gros Ventre Campground. The police had traced the vehicle to a man named Mitchell Warden, from the same county as Justin Barts. They still had no leads on the third man who'd been involved in the attacks at the ranch.

A shadow crossed Jesse's face as he shook his head. "The chief ranger told me this morning that search teams in the area were unable to track down any leads. They suspect he got a ride from one of his associates. Which means..."

"You want me to stick around a little longer."

"Hey, don't look so disappointed." He flashed her a grin, the kind that used to make her insides melt. Still would, if she hadn't built such a barricade around her heart. With guard towers. And a moat. "Think of it as a field trip. A day in the life of a park ranger."

"Sounds better than a day in the life of a rancher right now," she grumbled.

After breakfast, she followed Jesse back to headquarters, hovering around like a shadow while he tackled some paperwork at his desk. After a stint at the visitor center handing out backcountry passes, he led the way to his NPS vehicle, and they headed out on an afternoon patrol.

She couldn't help scanning the road as they drove up Teton Park Road, continually checking the mirrors and glancing at the turnouts they passed. Now that the SUV had been compounded by the police, would the men find another vehicle? Or was there a chance, however small, that they'd give up? And would the police be able to connect them to the real perpetrator? Because she didn't believe for a minute that some random men from Casper had decided to come attack her out of the blue.

The mountains loomed to the left—jagged, rocky peaks jutting seven thousand feet from the valley like they'd been dropped out of the brilliant blue sky. Snow covered most of the summits year-round, and clear glacial lakes dotted the base of the mountains, mirroring green forests rising to the tree line. She was reminded again how much she loved this place.

As she gazed out the window, Jesse glanced at her, a small smile on his lips. "You never get tired of it, do you?"

"Never." She bit her lip. "Did you miss it? When you left?"

A muscle worked in his jaw, and for a moment she thought that he wouldn't answer. That maybe she'd tapped into memories he'd rather leave untouched.

"I missed a lot of things, Sadie. I... It was..." He shook his head. "I'm sorry." His gaze connected with hers for the briefest moment before he faced forward again, but the emotions she saw in those blue eyes nearly stole her breath. Maybe he regretted what had he'd done as much as she did. "I let some other people influence me, and I shouldn't have. I should have decided for myself. I wish I could tell you how I sorry I really am."

Her throat went suddenly dry, and she swallowed. She hadn't meant to take the conversation this direction, but she appreciated his honesty. A hundred questions pressed against her mind. *Who said something to you? Why did you listen? Why wasn't what we had enough?* But she couldn't ask those things, not without leading them even deeper into the past and into a place of vulnerability she intended to avoid. She'd always thought his uncle had something to do with what happened, maybe fueled by the rift between Rob and her father. But why would Jesse have let that come between them? And why wouldn't he tell her back then, when she'd pressed him for answers?

"I believe you," she said after a moment. *I forgive you.* The words were right there, as if they wanted to be said aloud, but she couldn't. Wouldn't. Because that was way too close to deliberately tearing down the wall and draining the moat around her heart, and she wasn't ready for that. Not after she'd picked up all the pieces and carried on alone for so long. It was far safer—easier—to avoid conflict and relational drama altogether. "It's in the past, Jesse. We all do things we regret, and we have to pick ourselves up and move on. God has a way of working things for the good."

His gaze darted back to her again, blue eyes studying her for a second before turning back to the road. That muscle ticked in his jaw, almost as if he were chewing on her words. Did he believe her that she'd moved on?

Did it...bother him?

Nope, not even going to think that question. Because his feelings about her didn't matter anymore. And she *did* believe that God worked all things for the good—eventually. He just expected her to do her part to make the good things happen.

Too bad she'd been failing to live up to her end of the bargain lately. Otherwise, her ranch wouldn't be suffering the way it was. She needed to double down on her focus, meet with Mike, and figure out the best plan to move forward. *Without* letting herself get distracted.

"Move on. Right," Jesse said, interrupting her thoughts. He didn't look at her, just kept his eyes straight ahead as he drove. They spent the next couple of hours checking campsites, picnic areas, and trailheads. Toward late afternoon, he turned the vehicle onto a narrow dirt road leading toward the base of the mountains. After a moment of thick silence, he cleared his throat. "Last stop on our patrol is Lupine Meadows trailhead. I usually park and hang around for twenty minutes or so to answer questions, check the facilities and assist anyone if needed."

Jesse swung the SUV into an empty spot in the lot.

He shut the engine off, then turned to her. "You're welcome to come with me, or you can hang out here in the car."

"I think I'll try to connect with Mike Schmidt again, if it's all right with you. He was in meetings all morning." She dug her phone out of her pocket and flashed it at him. "We're still in cell service range here."

"Sounds good." He settled a park ranger hat on his head, then opened the door and climbed out.

Her eyes strayed to his back as he headed toward the signs at the trailhead. For so many years she'd seen him in denim and flannel. The park ranger uniform was a drastic change, and yet it suited him, emphasizing his broad shoulders and giving him an air of authority.

She'd be fine here for a few minutes. She'd call Mike, then see if the insurance company had received the police report yet. And check in with Zeke and Katrina.

Sadie opted to start with the easiest call first—Zeke. After he'd reassured her the ranch—and Kip—were fine, the patrol officer was still there, and Orion had been cooperating, she called Katrina.

She'd updated Katrina once or twice already, and now her friend nearly blew out her eardrum when she heard Sadie was in the national park with Jesse. The trouble was, her outburst sounded *happy* rather than upset.

"I'm glad he's taking care of you," Katrina said. "Somebody needs to. Do the police have any leads yet?"

"No, but they're looking into Amos Johnson next door and Stanley Fitz."

"The senator? My brother interned for him back in college. Said he was a good man." Katrina spoke the words thoughtfully, then her tone shifted. "But you know how it is with politicians—they're good at keeping up appearances. Keep me posted, okay?"

Sadie promised she would, then phoned Mike. Thankfully, this time he answered on the second ring.

"Hi, Mike, it's Sadie Madsen," she said.

"Sadie, great to hear from you." His voice came through a little tinny and garbled, but she could make out most of what he was saying. "I've been worried ever since I got your message. What happened?"

"I'll explain in person. I'm hoping we can set up another meeting?"

"Sure," he said, "let me patch you back to Dana to get that set up."

"Wait, Mike, quick question first. Do you know what charity Dad picked as the benefactor for the trust, if something happens to me?" She picked at her fingernails.

"Let me look that up for you, okay, Sadie? I don't know offhand, but I'll get that right away."

"Okay, thanks, Mike." She waited as the call transferred to his office assistant, who scheduled her for an afternoon meeting in two days. Hopefully he'd call before then with the name of the charity, so she could pass it along to the police. Or maybe she could find a copy of the trust at home in her father's files. It had to be there, somewhere.

The insurance company was last. She punched her way through the maze of the automated system, only to end up on hold. The music was painfully dull jazz in an endless loop, almost like they'd chosen it expressly for the purpose of infuriating their customers. She let out a slow sigh, her gaze drifting to the trailhead.

No sign of Jesse yet. The parking lot had gained a few more cars since they'd pulled in, and out on the main road, another vehicle turned onto the side road leading to the lot. She watched it drive slowly down the dirt road, a beat-up green Ford Bronco that looked old enough it could've belonged to her grandfather. When the automated system told her that her estimated hold time was forty-eight minutes, she clicked the red button to end the call. Forget it, she'd try again later.

As she stuffed her cell back into her pocket, she scanned the lot again. A family of hikers leaving the trail walked past her open door—parents with two young kids on foot and a baby on the father's back. The sight of them laughing together made something ache inside her chest. They paused behind her car, then crossed when the Bronco stopped for them. Sadie's gaze drifted to the vehicle. Suddenly, she froze. Every nerve in her body fired on full alarm, because that was Justin Barts in the passenger seat. The man who'd hunted them inside her pole barn. She was sure of it.

She slumped lower in her seat, praying he hadn't seen her. If he had, surely he'd be jumping out of the vehicle by now... But how had they known to look for her here? Or was it merely random chance?

The real question was, what to do now? She couldn't sit here waiting for Jesse, not if those men decided to search the lot. The presence of other people might deter them from harming her, but she wasn't willing to take that risk.

She peeked between the headrest and the seat at the

spot the Bronco had now driven past. Maybe they'd keep going and leave.

The knot in her chest tightened as the green SUV pulled over to one side, and both doors on the passenger side opened. She had to go, *now.*

Up the trail toward Jesse, and if she still had cell reception, she'd call the authorities on her way. The odds of losing them in the woods were far better than waiting in this vehicle like a sitting duck.

She slipped out of the passenger side and pressed the door shut. A glance at the Bronco showed the men were taking their sweet time getting out. Good.

She scurried for the trailhead, keeping to the shadows of the trees and ducking behind other hikers whenever possible.

The Bronco's doors slammed shut behind her. If they went straight for the trailhead, she had only the narrowest of head starts.

As her feet pounded up the trail, scanning the path ahead for any sign of a park ranger uniform, she heard a shout behind her. Her heart dropped into her shoes as she took off toward Jesse.

He should've gone back to tell Sadie what he was doing. Jesse chewed the inside of his cheek, scanning the forest along both sides of the trail and mentally kicking himself. He'd only meant to make a short trip.

A woman at the trailhead had told him she'd spotted a grizzly bear ten minutes earlier right off the trail. But twenty minutes had passed with no sign of the animal— no crushed foliage or broken branches, no scat, no tracks, no bear. If he didn't find the animal in the next few minutes, he'd *have* to turn around. Either it had moved on, or it had only been a deer mistaken for a bear in an excited hiker's mind.

He rounded another switchback, climbing a steeper section of the trail. Footsteps thumped on the packed earth behind him, and he turned to find Sadie half jogging, half speedwalking up the path behind him.

"Jesse," she gasped as she approached. "Thank goodness, I found you." She pressed a hand to her chest, breathing heavily from exertion.

Automatically he glanced behind her. The path was clear, but from the expression on her face, fear had propelled her up the hill. "What happened? What's going on?"

"Barts. The other men." She sucked in a breath. "At least three of them. They're in an old Ford Bronco instead of the blue Explorer. I think they spotted me."

He placed his hands on her shoulders, tilting his head down to hold her wide-eyed gaze. "You saw them? Where, in the lot?"

She nodded, then took a few deep breaths. "I didn't want to risk getting caught, so I took off up the trail to find you."

"Did you call the po—" He cut off at the sound of footsteps, pressing a finger to his lips. It *could* be more hikers, but they wouldn't know until whoever it was moved into sight. By then, it might be too late.

Sadie glanced rapidly between him and the trail behind her. He waved for her to follow, then led the way up to the next switchback. A large boulder stood at the inside of the bend. She ducked behind it, crouching out of sight, while Jesse squatted next to her, peering around the edge. One hand rested on the rough rock, the other on the gun tucked into his belt. Lethal force was the very last option he'd use, but if their lives hung in the balance, he wouldn't hesitate.

He held his breath, waiting. When his radio crackled, he switched it off as adrenaline flooded his veins. Farther down the trail, color flashed between the trees—black and dark blue, a pop of white and red. *Please be hikers.* Two men strode around the bend, their faces obscured by cowboy hats. Not typical hiking apparel. His chest tightened.

Then voices carried up the mountainside, indistinct at first but becoming clear as they approached. "You sure she went this far? Maybe she's hiding off the trail somewhere back there."

"I would've seen her tracks. I ain't stupid, Barts. Who's the best hunter this side of the Tetons? Me."

Jesse ducked back behind the rock, assessing their options. Sadie's brown eyes watched him, her whole body rigid. Staying here was out of the question. The area was too exposed to attempt hiding immediately off trail. Neither did he want to risk a confrontation with the two men while hikers were out here. Undoubtedly both men were armed, and they wouldn't have any qualms about shooting to kill.

Their best alternative was to keep going uphill and then veer off into the woods as soon as they came to a decent hiding place. He caught Sadie's gaze, then pointed up the trail. At first her eyes widened, but then she nodded, apparently reaching the same conclusion he had. He waved her forward, gesturing for her to stay low.

She pushed off the rock and crept up the path. Jesse followed, keeping close behind her, his hand hovering near his gun. His heart thrummed like the pistons in a race car as his boots crunched over loose dirt and gravel. Voices still carried uphill from the men below, louder now, as if they were arguing.

"Oh, come off it, Davis. You're the one who let her get away last time."

"Ha, me? That was all Warden and his terrible driving. Serves him right, cops got his car."

At least the men were being loud enough they wouldn't hear Jesse's and Sadie's footsteps. He glanced around, searching for a decent hiding place. It wouldn't be much farther before the subalpine forest ended and the trail would ascend the mountainside up into Garnet Canyon in a series of fully exposed switchbacks.

Ahead of him, Sadie caught the toe of her boot on a rock and stumbled. He grabbed her arm, tugging her upright.

"Did you hear that?" said the man named Davis.

Jesse and Sadie froze, exchanging wide-eyed glances. They had to get to cover. *Stat.* That clump of bushes up ahead would be a good start, if they could just get around it and get down. The sun had vanished behind the mountains, swathing the forest in dark shadow. Sweat beaded his forehead as he dragged Sadie past the bushes and off the trail, flopping to his stomach next to her on the ground behind the thick foliage. Pine needles and small rocks bit into his palms as he pressed his hands against the ground, eyes on the trail just visible through the low branches.

Boots thumped up the path—he could feel it more than hear it—and he held his breath, waiting for them to pass.

The wind whispered through the trees high above, the only sound beyond the thudding of his heart in his ears and the movement of the men. Sadie huddled close, her face tucked into the dirt like she couldn't bear to watch. Then two pairs of legs hiked past, heading upward. It wouldn't take them long, though, to see what he'd seen—that the trail soon became too exposed to hide. They'd turn around and come back.

Jesse tapped Sadie's arm, and she looked up at him, softly brushing dirt off her cheek.

"We have to go," he whispered. "They'll be coming back down before long. Follow me."

He rose to a crouch, then kept low as he worked his way between the trees, heading downhill roughly perpendicular to the section of the path they'd just left, and parallel to the curve of the descending trail below the boulder where they'd first taken cover. The terrain was steep enough they had to use caution or else they'd end up sliding twenty or thirty feet and alerting the entire mountain to their presence.

Once they'd gone far enough that the trail was well out of sight, Jesse stopped, visually noting some landmarks to keep his bearings. Now he could turn around without losing track of the right direction to reach the trail. He glanced upward, surveying the cracks of sky peeking through the treetops above. Wispy white clouds streaked against the deep blue of late afternoon.

"What do we do?" Sadie asked, using the break to brush pine needles and dirt from her clothes. "I saw two guys get out, which means the third one is still down at the trailhead."

"Did you get the chance to call the cops?"

She shook her head. "I was afraid they'd hear me, and then I lost service. Radio?"

"Too risky yet. It's loud." He glared at the sky. "It'll be evening soon. If we find a sheltered spot, we can wait them out."

Sadie shivered, then tucked her hands inside her pockets.

A sudden, fierce urge swept over him to pull her into his arms, but after the way she'd responded to him earlier, he didn't dare. When he'd offered that attempt at an apology, she'd made it more than clear she'd moved on. Maybe it would've made a difference if he could've explained exactly what happened, how out of nowhere her father had flat-out told him he wasn't good enough for her and accused him of being a gold digger after the ranch, but he wouldn't do that to her memory of Dale. After everything else he'd taken from her, he couldn't take that away, too. Especially when those words had been so unfounded, so brutally painful.

And when he'd given in and broken things off with her, he'd only felt like he'd proved Dale's words: *You'll never be enough for my daughter.* But was it any different than what Rob had drilled into him? He didn't need Sadie confirming their assessment by rejecting him, too. No, it was far better to keep her at arm's length.

His throat grew thick, and he swallowed. "Come on," he said, waving her forward. "I know it's chilly out here. Let's try to find someplace a little more protected."

Ten minutes later, they hunkered down next to a couple of big trees with a thicket of brambles off to one side. Tiny, unripe, black raspberries taunted them from the thorny branches. In a few weeks, they'd grow plump and juicy instead of hard and red like they were now. His stomach growled at the thought.

He pressed his hand to his shirt, and Sadie snickered.

She glanced down at the black utility belt around his waist. "Got any snacks in there?"

"Like a mini vending machine? No such luck." He took off his hat, setting it to one side, then dug into one of the pouches on his belt. "I do have a flashlight, though. That'll come in handy once we can risk it."

Her eyes softened in the fading light. "Thank you, Jesse. I just want you to know how much I appreciate everything you're doing for me. I didn't want to drag you into this, but…" She sucked in a slow breath. "I couldn't have handled it on my own."

His heart beat a little faster, and this time it had nothing to do with armed pursuers. "You're welcome. I wasn't kidding earlier when I told you I would protect you."

She kept her gaze latched on his, and her throat bobbed.

He forced himself to go on, to ask the question that had been plaguing him. "Is there a chance you could forgive me? One day?"

More words hovered like mist on the edges of his mind, words he couldn't quite match with his feelings. Why did it matter so much? What did he want from her? Friendship? A second chance? No, he'd only run the risk of breaking her heart again. Or his own, this time, if she decided he wasn't enough for her after all. She'd meant the world to him once, but he couldn't allow that to happen again, for both their sakes.

She broke eye contact and looked down at her hands, rubbing the fingers of one hand against the palm of the other. "Jesse, I… I know God calls us to forgive, and I want to, but I don't know how to separate forgiving from trusting you again. I can *say* I forgive you, but I don't know how to mean it, in here." She rubbed her hand against her heart. "I still don't understand what happened to us." Her soft words wobbled on a choked breath.

Should I tell her? His insides twisted at the thought of how much pain he'd caused her. How much he'd lost by making the choice he'd made. At its root, that decision had been an act of fear, hadn't it? Fear that his uncle and Dale were right, and that he'd disappoint Sadie. That one day she'd wake up and see he *wasn't* good enough for her.

But God had put them in the same path again, for at least this short time. At least he could prove his trustworthiness now. He forced a smile to his lips. "It's a start."

She smiled back, tentatively, and a connection stretched between them like the thin silky filament of a spider's web. Then abruptly she jerked away, searching the woods across from where they sat, and Jesse heard it, too. A soft rustling of foliage.

Adrenaline fired through his veins. Had the men found them? He scrambled to his feet, pulling Sadie up next to him. The sound was coming from lower down the mountain, not the way they'd come. Maybe they could retreat uphill.

A snuffling, snorting sound stopped him before he'd taken a step, and the hairs stood up on the back of his neck. In the last of the fading daylight, something large and brown lumbered toward them between the trees. Not the men.

The grizzly bear.

SEVEN

Sadie clapped her hand over her mouth to keep quiet as the massive bear came closer, nosing at the ground. It paused, lifting its head and swiveling beady, dark eyes around the forest as it sniffed the air. When it picked up their scent, it froze, staring in their direction.

Instinct told her to run, but after living her entire life near the mountains, she knew better. Running might trigger a chase response.

Jesse's firm hand on her arm said the same thing.

"Stand up, nice and slow," he whispered, then helped her to her feet. Her legs felt unnaturally wobbly, like spaghetti noodles instead of solid bone and muscle. His other hand reached down to his utility belt and came away with a canister of bear spray. He had a gun, too—they weren't defenseless—but her fight-or-flight system hadn't gotten the message.

The bear's ears lay back flat against its head. It made a short huffing, blowing sound that echoed through the quiet forest and made Sadie's knees shake. She'd faced wild animals before on the ranch, but usually it was wolves or coyotes from behind the barrel of a rifle and twenty yards' distance. Not a six-hundred-pound grizzly at twenty *feet*.

"We need to back away," Jesse said softly.

"Where?" Their backs were literally against trees. Bark dug into her spine.

He pointed to a narrow gap between a trunk and some undergrowth on his left, heading uphill. "That way. Go behind me. Backward, so you're still facing the bear."

Jesse shuffled forward, creating a gap between him and the tree and raising his arms at his sides in a protective shield.

Her feet didn't want to cooperate, but somehow she forced one boot sideways, then the other.

The bear stared at them, its head swaying back and forth.

She backed up slowly toward the gap, resting a hand on the nearest trunk to keep from tripping on exposed roots. Branches tugged at her shirt and scraped against her jeans as she kept backing away. Soon she'd cleared the patch of undergrowth and stood once more on the open forest floor. The bear was still visible as fuzzy glimpses of brown between the trees, but she couldn't see its face anymore.

"Keep going, still backward," Jesse said, "until it's out of sight."

It hadn't moved. That was good—it wasn't following them. She kept sliding her boots backward up the hillside, shuffling through pine needles and dead leaves, feeling gingerly for exposed rocks or roots that might take her down and draw the grizzly's attention.

After what felt like an eternity, Jesse stopped. He stood still for a long moment, listening, then turned to her. The worry lines relaxed around his eyes. "I think we're clear now. Good job."

She let out a long, slow breath. "Thanks, you, too. I'm glad you had the spray."

"I'm glad we didn't have to use it." He tucked it back into his belt.

Suddenly she pointed at his head. "Your hat, did you leave it?"

He reached for the top of his head, fingers running over his hair. "Looks like the bear gets it."

"Better the hat than us. Now what? Is it safe to head back?" The temperature had plunged as the sun slipped toward the western horizon, and she stuffed chilly fingers into her jeans pockets. It was going to be a cold night.

One of his arms lifted, almost as if he were going to wrap it around her, but then he dropped it to his side. Disappointment wreathed her insides, despite her better judgment. "They might have given up. Or they might be waiting for us to reappear lower down the trail." He looked around in the growing darkness, as if gauging their location and trying to decide. "It's almost dark. We can't risk using a flashlight in case they're still out here, which means we won't make it all the way back to the parking lot. I think our best option is to find another spot to wait it out."

"If we go farther up, we'll get out of bear territory, right?"

"Yeah, up past the tree line. Come on."

She followed as he led the way uphill until they reached the trail nearly where they'd left it. There was no sign of motion, and the only sounds came from a gentle breeze and the rustling of small animals. As they stepped out onto the trail, she half expected someone to open fire, but nothing happened.

Instead they hiked in near silence up to the next switchback, where the trees gave way to rocky, exposed mountainside and the lights of Jackson sparkled far below like tiny pieces of glitter on the valley floor. Night quickly consumed the last rays of daylight, making the sky look as if someone had splashed blue and black watercolor paint across it. Sadie trudged after Jesse, concentrating on her footing and keeping her huffing breath as quiet as she could. Her mouth grew dry and parched with thirst, and her empty stomach gurgled.

Finally, after a few more switchbacks, the trail spilled out onto the saddle between two of the mountains. A boulder field stretched upward, forming the base of the canyon and leading up steep ascents to the jagged snowcapped peaks. The last of the light had faded, revealing a million stars twinkling overhead. The air smelled of crisp, cold snow, and fog puffed from her mouth with each breath.

Jesse touched her arm and pointed to a couple of large boulders wedged next to each other nearby. When she gave him a thumbs-up, he led the way over, picking a careful path through the rocks. This place was a sprained ankle waiting to happen in this low light, but at least they didn't have to worry about snakes at this elevation.

They found a decently flat rock sheltered on two sides. Sadie sat next to Jesse, keeping space between them despite the chilly night air. That had been one good thing about hiking—moving had kept her warm. Now there was only cold rock beneath her and behind her.

"Here." Jesse pressed a metal bottle into her hands. "It's all the water I've got unless we find a stream."

She took the bottle and unscrewed the thick cap fitted with a filter system. A few precious mouthfuls chipped away at the edge of her thirst but did nothing to help the empty feeling in her stomach. Then she passed the bottle back and hugged her knees to her chest, fighting off the shivers trying to make her teeth chatter.

And poor Jesse. She realized as she watched him screw the cap back onto the bottle that he was wearing short sleeves. It had to be less than fifty degrees up here by now, with the temperature rapidly dropping. Daytime highs this time of year were often in the low seventies, but at night, the lows could plunge into the thirties.

He didn't complain, didn't pressure her into huddling together for body warmth. Just rubbed his hands up and down his arms for a moment before tucking the bottle back into the utility belt at his waist.

Something twinged inside her chest at his selfless care for her. In many ways, he was the same man now that he'd been so many years ago. Responsible, caring, concerned for others' welfare—especially hers—generous. He'd been more upbeat and positive back then, as if the worries of life had worn away some of his optimism since that time.

Of course, given the extreme situation they were in, maybe now wasn't the right time to analyze his personality.

She did know this—there was no reason to make the poor man suffer any more than he had to, especially on her behalf. "Is it okay if I slide closer? For warmth? You look like you're freezing."

"Fine with me," he said it with a slight stutter, as if fighting off chattering teeth the same way she was. "Sorry a fire isn't an option."

"That's okay." She shuffled closer to him, tucking in against his side the way she would've years ago if they were watching a movie together. He wrapped his arm around her, and when her fingers brushed his cold skin, she draped her arm over his and let her head lean against his shoulder. Despite the cold air biting the tip of her nose, the rest of her felt snuggly and warm. She stared up at the stars for a long time, listening to the sound of Jesse's breath as it matched the rise and fall of his chest, until her eyes grew heavy.

It felt like only minutes later that he was shifting next to her, and she pried thick eyelids open to see that the boulder field was visible once more in the milky dawn spreading from the east. She pulled away, sorry to lose the delicious sense of warmth, and shook her numb limbs.

"Sorry for waking you," he said, his mouth twisting in a wry grin, "but I was losing feeling in my legs."

She smiled. "Me, too. But hey, we survived the night."

"I'm sorry that was even in question." He stood, then held out a hand to help her up. "We've got enough light now we can try descending."

Sadie followed him back across the boulder field, picking her way carefully toward the canyon entrance. The sky grew gradually lighter in the east as the sun inched its way up behind the Gros Ventre range on the opposite side of the valley. Jesse paused where the boulder field gave way to dirt trail, scanning the path ahead.

"Do you think—"

A sharp crack cut her short, and something pinged against a boulder behind her near the canyon entrance, sending a spray of rock chips pelting into the back of her head and neck.

"Down!" Jesse dove for her, half tackling her to the trail as she dropped to her stomach on the dirt. More gunshots fired, biting into the edge of the canyon wall.

She tucked herself into a ball against the nearest rock, covering her head. "Where are they?"

"Above us, up the canyon." A muscle ticked in Jesse's jaw as he clenched his teeth. His hand slipped to his waist and came up with his gun. "See up there? Motion on the ridge. Looks like two of them."

She squinted, straining to see in the faint early morning light. Then two shapes resolved themselves, darker blobs against the dark mass of rock, scrambling in their direction.

"Sadie, you have to go," he said. "Keep to the trail as long as you can, then call the police as soon as you get in cell range."

Her stomach knotted up like a noose. "What about you?"

He released the safety on the gun. "I'm going to hold them off. I'll follow as soon as it's safe."

Up on the ridge, the two men paused.

"Now, before they start firing again!"

Her lungs felt like they'd turned to steel, incapable of breath, as she slowly backed away from him. Crawling on hands and knees, she scrambled for the trail. Only a few feet, and she'd be safely out of range outside the canyon entrance.

The men opened fire, bullets biting into the rocks to her right. Jesse fired back, but only a few shots—probably to give her time to escape rather than an attempt to injure. Then she was out on the trail, and Jesse and the men vanished from view. There was only the outer wall of the canyon to her right and the open vista of the Hole on her left. She scrambled to her feet, then took off down the narrow path.

Her heart stuttered more than once as she slipped on loose dirt. The descent was more treacherous than last night's climb had been. More gunfire rang out behind her, spurring her forward. *Please protect Jesse, Lord.*

She raced toward the next switchback, slowing to take

the turn safely. But despite her caution, her boot caught a patch of loose gravel. Her heart leaped into her throat as her foot slid, the momentum carrying her toward the exposed edge of the trail. She fought to regain her balance, then exhaled a breath of relief when she caught herself just at the edge of a precipitous drop. That would've been a long fall.

Then the rock under her feet gave way, and there was nothing beneath her boots but empty space.

Jesse fired off another shot, hoping to buy Sadie enough time to escape. Up above, the two dark shapes on the ridge had vanished from view as they worked their way down to where he hid. He reached for his radio, flipping it back on with a crackle of static. No reason to hide now. In fact, if the two men heard him, maybe it would be enough to scare them into running.

"Dispatch, this is Ranger Jesse Taylor. Copy?"

"Copy, Ranger Taylor. What's your 10-20? We've got a team searching for you."

"Garnet Canyon entrance. You need to close Lupine Meadow tr—"

A scream split the air, and every cell in his body froze. *Sadie.*

But then another shot fired, so close he could hear the bullet whistling past. Adrenaline flooded his veins as he pulled back, pressing himself against the canyon wall. He took a couple of breaths to calm his heart rate, then stole a glance back to the ridge and the boulder field.

The men were right there, scrambling over rocks, heading straight for him. He gritted his teeth; he had no choice but to shoot. Bullets bit into the rock a few feet away, and he ducked back. Wiped a palm on his pants.

He took a steadying breath, tightened his grip on the gun and swiveled toward the approaching men. Aiming for the closest dark shape, he squeezed the trigger as bullets whistled past him.

A low grunt told him the bullet had found its mark, and one of the men went down. He aimed for the other man. "Drop your weapon. National Park Service. You're under arrest."

He couldn't make out the man's face in the dim light, but the way he froze was unmistakable. The man's head swiveled toward his fallen friend, then back toward Jesse. He stood immobile for a split second, as if in indecision, then lobbed his gun back up the boulder field and took off, scrambling for the nearest cover.

Jesse grabbed his radio, then quickly updated the dispatcher on the situation. They already had a team at the trailhead lot, where they'd found his NPS vehicle in the middle of the night. A medical evac team would take care of the injured man. Right now, his priority was to get to Sadie and make sure she was safe.

He reset the safety on his gun and tucked it back into the holster, then took off down the trail. The light was growing, turning the sky into rainbow sherbet in the east, but there was no sign of Sadie. Tension knotted in his gut as he surveyed the trail below, where the section after the switchback was visible from above. No sign of her.

"Sadie!" he called.

"Help! I'm down here!" A muffled yell from up ahead reached his ears. His throat constricted as he dashed toward the switchback. Fresh damage to the trail edge told him what had happened—she'd gone over.

Dropping to his knees, he looked over the edge. "Sadie!"

She dangled maybe six feet below, her hands wrapped around a scrawny tree tenaciously growing from the steep mountain face. At the sound of her name, she looked up, her pale face streaked with dirt.

"I can't hold on much longer!" she gasped.

He fumbled in his utility belt, pulling out a coil of paracord. "Don't you let go, Sadie Madsen. I'll get you up." His fingers, stiff with cold, didn't want to cooperate, but he forced them to make a small loop on one end, dangling a couple of carabiners from it to weigh it down. The other end, he wrapped around his waist and knotted securely into place. "I'm lowering a loop of paracord. You need to get one of your feet into it. Can you do that?"

"I… I don't—"

"Yes, you can." He tossed the loop over the edge, guiding the carabiners close to her leg. "It's near your left shin. Pull that boot up and slide it in."

"Can that hold my weight?"

"It's military grade, rated to five hundred and fifty pounds."

She fumbled with her foot, struggling to find the loop, but finally the paracord went taut as she slid her boot in. "Okay. Now what?"

"Place your other foot on top of that one, outside the loop. Then you've got to switch your hands over to the cord, one at a time. I've got you, you won't fall." He infused his voice with confidence even though every nerve in his body buzzed with fear. All it took was one miscalculation, one missed grip, one loss of balance… The voices of his uncle and Dale drifted through his head, but he shut them out. Surviving the outdoors, helping people—this was what he did. What he was good at.

He wound the cord in front of his waist around his hands, bracing his feet against a rock embedded into the trail. Below, she still clung tightly to the tree. He held his breath as she swung one hand over and gripped the skinny cord. Then, the other, and the cord around his hands and waist jerked taut, digging into his skin through the fabric of his uniform. He had to lean back against her weight, making it impossible to see over the edge.

"Pull!" she yelled.

Every tendon and muscle in his arms strained as he hauled on the thin line. Pulling it tight with his left hand, he loosened his right and slid it down the length of paracord, then brought his left down to his right. Over and over again, inches at a time, he heaved the line as the cord bit into his skin, until finally Sadie's blond head appeared over the edge.

Once he'd pulled her high enough, she released the paracord with one hand and hooked her fingers over a rock jutting out of the trail. Careful not to release the line, he knelt and grasped her other hand, then pulled her up the rest of the way until they both collapsed backward onto the trail, chests heaving in the early dawn light.

After a long moment, Jesse got to his knees. He brushed a loose strand of hair away from Sadie's face. "Hey, are you all right?"

She sat up, glancing around almost as if in a daze. Finally her gaze landed on the broken trail edge, and she blinked away the glossiness forming in her eyes. "I wasn't even going that fast. Just hit a patch of loose dirt and—" she shrugged, turning those wide brown eyes up to him "—*boom*, over the edge. Just like that. If you hadn't been here…"

The words hit his chest like a knife. He'd come so close

to losing her, after just finding her again. Why, oh why, had he ever left her in the first place? "Sadie—" Heat built in his throat, and he swallowed. Feelings that had long lain dormant swirled beneath his ribs, threatening to break free.

"I can't keep doing this, Jesse," she whispered. "I just... I'm not strong enough."

He shook his head. "No, Sadie. You are the strongest person I've ever met. I watched you work with your parents for years. And now, the things you're doing at the ranch with so little help? Your perseverance blows me away."

Something shifted in her expression. Maybe it was the faintest upturn of her lips or the softening of her gaze as she looked at him with those big brown eyes. Not a solid color like a deer's, but multiple shades of brown and gold, complex and rich like a perfect cup of coffee.

He leaned closer, studying the depths of her gaze. When she shifted onto her knees, he stretched tentative fingers to her cheek and smoothed away flecks of dirt. Somehow they'd gotten closer, mere inches of space separating them as they breathed the same air. Their years apart had only served to show him what he'd given up. She'd become even more beautiful, in form and in spirit, with her dedication to her family's legacy and her care for those around her— both people and animals.

When her gaze dropped to his lips, he cupped his hand against her cheek, then leaned forward and pressed his mouth to hers. For a few perfect seconds, the world and all its grief and danger and regret vanished. There were only the two of them, the way things were meant to be.

Then Sadie pulled back, pressing a hand against her lips. Into the vacuum between them rushed all the things he'd done wrong. All the ways he'd failed her. All the mean things her father had said.

And now he was doing it again, kissing her when she'd expressly stated she wanted to move on. *And* against his better judgment. Bringing feelings into their tentative friendship was a *terrible* idea. If he opened up his heart to her, and she rejected him the way Dale and his uncle had... He wanted nothing to do with that kind of pain again. Far better to stick with what he knew he was good at—like work. Not relationships.

"I—" she started, then clamped her mouth shut and pushed to her feet. "We should get going."

"Yes," he agreed, keeping his focus anywhere but on her and fighting the urge to blurt an apology that would only make things more awkward. He brushed his hands against his pants, wincing as raw skin rubbed against the heavy fabric. The paracord had dug into his palms, chafing the skin to raw bright red patches in places.

"Your hands," Sadie said, and when he dared a quick glance up, he caught her throat bobbing.

"They're fine." Maybe not *exactly* the truth, but he'd survive. He busied himself winding up the paracord and stowing it and the carabiners back in his belt. "Let's get going. One of the men is incapacitated, but the other ran. We don't want to be up here still if he changes his mind." The words came out more brusquely than he'd intended, and he found he couldn't meet Sadie's eye.

Silence weighed on his shoulders as they hiked back down the trail. When he reached the place they'd left the trail to hide the night before, where they'd encountered the bear, he made a mental note of the location. He'd have to report that, too. He pulled the water bottle from his belt and handed it to Sadie. After they'd each had a few sips, he tucked it away again.

In the distance, the soft, rhythmic thumps of a helicopter rotor beat through the air.

The sun had crested the mountains in the east by the time they reached the parking lot. Morning dew glistened on the surrounding fields. Two ranger vehicles had appeared, and they'd set up cones at the turnoff to the main road to keep visitors from coming to the trailhead. A few cars remained from multiday backpackers, but otherwise the lot was clear. No sign of the Bronco Sadie had told him about.

The chief ranger hailed him as they walked toward his vehicle. "Jesse!" Whit jogged over, then scoured the two of them with his gaze. "Ranger Taylor, Ms. Madsen, I can't tell you how glad we are to see you both."

"And you all are a sight for sore eyes." Jesse offered a wide grin, thinking again how blessed he was to work for someone as good-natured as Whit Morgan. He had to admit, there had been a few silver linings to coming back here. Maybe more than a few if he was being honest. "What's the status?"

"The green Bronco was gone by the time we found your vehicle at three a.m. We'll keep monitoring the area for it in case the driver comes back to pick up his compadres. A helitack crew is on the way for the injured man, and they're bringing up a few Jenny Lake rangers to track the one who escaped. I also redirected the crew that was searching for you to join the hunt."

"I heard the chopper." Jesse glanced up at the sky, where small fluffy clouds dotted the brilliant morning blue. "I hope we can get some answers." His gaze landed on Sadie's, and for a second something sparked between them—

shared, common purpose and memories of their frigid night under the stars. For a moment, it felt like it was the two of them against the world. Then he remembered how *he* was the one who'd broken faith and left her to face the world alone. The massive block of his guilt wedged between them, and he couldn't look at her anymore.

They followed the chief ranger back to headquarters, where Jesse tended to his injured hands and the office staff managed to pull together an impromptu breakfast of day-old donuts, protein bars, orange juice and coffee. He and Sadie tucked in like they hadn't eaten in weeks. He'd always appreciated that about her—she never balked at a meal. Probably because she also never balked at work or effort or exercise.

By the time they'd finished recounting everything that had happened, the helitack team notified Whit that they'd apprehended the injured man and were en route to the hospital. No word yet on the escapee. Jesse absorbed the information, glancing at Sadie. She'd want to go home, no doubt, now that at least part of the threat was gone. But she couldn't keep living this way, constantly watching over her shoulder. It was time they did some investigating on their own, and he had a sneaking suspicion he knew exactly who could help them.

"Chief Morgan," he said as they wrapped up the conversation, "I'd like to take you up on that offer of a few days off. I think I might be able to help Sadie figure out who's behind these attacks."

Her eyebrows shot up, then pulled together. From the slight downturn to her lips, she wasn't exactly thrilled about more time together. *Tough.* This wasn't about him and her or their past, this was about preserving her future.

"Of course, Ranger Taylor," Whit said. "Take the time you need and stay safe."

Sadie followed Jesse outside and back to his house, her mouth sealed shut in a remarkable display of restraint. He kept expecting her to object any moment, but she waited patiently in his living room as he changed out of his uniform and threw together an overnight bag. When he walked back out to her with the duffel over his shoulder, she stood to face him, hands on her hips.

"Jesse, what are you doing?"

"I'm taking you back to the ranch."

She shook her head. "No, the bag. What are you doing?"

"You're in danger." He rammed a hand through his hair. "And I'm not letting you out of my sight until you're safe. We're not going to sit back and play defense anymore."

Her lips quirked to one side for a split second before she forced them back to neutral. "Oh yeah? What are *we* going to do instead?"

"We're going to take this investigation into our own hands, and I know just the man we need to see."

"And who's that?" Her posture shifted, becoming less defensive as her shoulders relaxed, and he knew he'd won.

Except that the man they had to go see was probably the *last* person he wanted to visit.

"My uncle Rob."

EIGHT

This was a bad idea. The thought kept rattling through Sadie's brain the entire way back to her ranch. And as she greeted Kip and updated the Nelsons on everything that had happened. *And* while she packed her own bag to bring along on the trip to Jackson Hole. Just in case, Jesse told her.

She'd never cared much for Rob Clark, especially since he'd fallen out with her father while she and Jesse were dating. He'd always come across as a little too selfish and cutthroat in his business tactics. That opinion had only been reinforced by the rift with her father. And she was still convinced Rob lay somewhere at the root of why Jesse had left.

But it wasn't Rob that was the problem now. It was Jesse.

It was the way he kept risking his own life to save hers. The way he insisted on sticking around despite the personal risks. It was his strong jawline, his sinewy forearms visible with his shirt cuffs rolled up, the feel of his lips against hers. How safe she felt when she was with him. It was even the way Kip had run up to him *before* he ran to Sadie.

On a scale of terrible ideas, kissing him ranked right up there with the time she volunteered to do a polar plunge for a church fundraiser. In the Snake River. In January.

And yet, she'd done it anyway. Maybe it had been inevitable from the first moment he'd pulled her out of the burning stable. At least, Katrina would say so—if Sadie could ever hit the pause button long enough to tell her friend the latest episode in the Sadie–Jesse saga.

And now she was voluntarily taking her "just in case" overnight bag and Kip to climb into his truck and go visit his uncle to look for answers.

She'd hoped Mike Schmidt might have left her a message with the name of the charity from the trust, but apparently he hadn't gotten around to checking yet. Maybe Rob would know.

Regardless, there would be absolutely no more kissing. No more noticing how Jesse had grown up and matured into a different person, one who was reliable to the point of risking his life. No more contemplating how things could've been different.

No more anything that might lead to feelings for him.

When he helped Kip up into the back of his truck without her needing to ask, she clenched her teeth.

"You okay?" he asked after they'd both climbed in and buckled. Her scowl must have been written across her forehead—not the best way to show appreciation.

She forced a smile. "Sure. Thanks for taking care of Kip."

"He's a good boy." Jesse glanced back at where Kip sat on the back seat. The collie let out a happy yip, as if returning the compliment. Kip loved car rides and, apparently, Jesse.

Sadie stifled the urge to groan. At least the post-kiss awkwardness had vanished now that they had a goal. He'd seemed as annoyed at himself as she had felt after it happened. Which was good—*great*—because that meant it wouldn't happen again.

Jesse started the truck and headed out onto the main road. Sadie shifted in her seat, glancing in the side mirror every few minutes, but no speeding car came swerving toward them. Just the usual empty road with an occasional passerby.

"The police called," he said after a few minutes. "The man I shot was Justin Barts."

"The guy from the pole barn."

"Right. He's been in surgery all morning, so they haven't been able to question him yet."

She sighed, running her fingers down her long braid where it rested on her shoulder. It had taken her a solid quarter of an hour to pick all the twigs and tangles out of her hair after their unplanned night on the trail. "He's not going to tell us anything."

One hand tightened on the steering wheel, then his fingers loosened. "Not while he's under anesthesia, that's for sure. But we have to try. Any word from your financial advisor about the charity named in the trust?"

"Not yet, but I'm hoping your uncle might know."

"Maybe." A muscle flexed in his cheek. No love lost between those two, a fact that apparently hadn't changed with time. It had to have been hard on him as a teen, losing his own father and ending up with his mother's brother instead. He hadn't talked much about it, but she'd witnessed their strained relationship back when they were dating, and the subtle control Rob exerted over Jesse.

"Was it Rob? Was he the one who talked you into leaving?" The question popped out before she could stop herself.

The vehicle went so silent she could hear her heart thudding in her ears.

A muscle flexed in Jesse's jaw. "I'd rather not talk about it, Sadie."

Disappointment washed over her, even though his reticence was probably for the best. What difference would it make now? She just needed to get through this investigation and get on with her life at the ranch. Forget Jesse Taylor and the unfortunate effects he had on her heart.

She watched out the window as the miles passed on their way into town. By the time they'd grabbed sandwiches at a deli and pulled up outside Rob's condo unit—probably worth millions given Jackson prices—the sun had peaked and started its long trek toward the west. Little cotton ball clouds hung over the mountains like someone had spilled a bag of them across the sky. They looked innocent enough right now, but odds were they'd build into thunderstorms later in the afternoon. This region was notorious for volatile weather.

Too much like Sadie's own emotions right now. She left a couple of windows cracked for Kip, then walked with Jesse toward the sleek, modern building. "This is an upgrade from his old place."

These units couldn't be more than a few years old. Uncle Rob was apparently doing pretty well for himself.

"He moved out of the other apartment when he sold the building. Guess you haven't been in touch with him?" Jesse's expression remained hooded.

"Nope. Other than when I run into him in a store every now and then. He's offered a few times to broker the deal for me if I ever decide to sell the ranch, so I guess there's that." At the way Jesse's eyebrows shot up, she held up a hand. "He's never been pushy about it."

"Hmm. Well, we'll see what he has to say." He buzzed

the front doorbell of his uncle's unit and slung a thumb in his front jeans pocket. No doubt about it, he'd only gotten more handsome with time.

She forced her attention away from the six-foot-two walking source of trouble next to her and instead studied the exterior of the building.

Then the door swung open, and Rob Clark offered them a polished smile that matched his gleaming shoes and pristinely cut attire. "Jesse! And Sadie Madsen. I'm so glad I had some free space in my schedule this afternoon."

Jesse winced as Rob pulled him into a stiff man hug and clapped his back before ushering them inside.

The interior reflected the same sophisticated style as the outside, a take on modern mountain living with nods to the region's past. A white brick fireplace took up one wall, stretching up to the two-story ceiling. Panoramic glass windows filled the adjoining wall, showcasing gorgeous views of the mountains. Rob had a collection of framed art showing historic Jackson buildings hanging above his black leather furniture set. It was tastefully done, but not at all to her preferences. She much preferred the stone and wood and rustic feel of the ranch. And with the fine-grain, unblemished leather and the immaculate laminate wood floors, she was glad she'd left Kip in the truck.

She and Jesse each took a chair on either side of a small marble end table.

"Can I get either of you a drink?" Rob offered, pointing to a polished wet bar built into a corner of the room near the fireplace.

"No, thanks," Jesse said as Sadie shook her head. Like her, he sat perched on the edge of the chair's firm cushion. "We don't want to take up much of your time." He waited for Rob to take a seat on the sofa, then went on, "As I mentioned in my text, there have been some concerning incidents recently at Sadie's ranch, and we're trying to get to the bottom of who might be behind things. We have our suspicions, but we'd like to hear your take."

Rob rubbed a hand across his chin. His salt-and-pepper hair was cut short and slicked neatly into place. The large rings on his hands reinforced the display of polished wealth, but his ring finger was empty. As far as she knew, he'd never been married. "I'll give it my best shot. Can you fill me in on what you know?"

Jesse glanced at Sadie, as if offering her the chance to speak, but she pressed her lips firmly together.

Please go ahead. She'd lived through each dreadful thing enough times already. His gaze lingered a moment, then he nodded and turned back to his uncle. Gratitude filled her chest as he recounted the events of the past few days, sharing the key parts and skimming over the rest.

"Since you know everyone around here, we were hoping you might have some insights," Jesse finished.

"That's a lot, Sadie. I'm glad you're okay." A crease settled between Rob's brows, and he stared past them out the windows toward the Tetons beyond. "The Double M has been attracting interest for years. Even when Dale was still alive, he was always receiving purchase offers. When I got into real estate, I offered to help him broker the deal in case he ever decided to sell, but he's always been committed to preserving the ranch for you and your family, Sadie." He glanced at her, but no flicker of extra awareness or emotion crossed his face, almost as if he'd forgotten what had happened between her and Jesse. Or maybe he just expected she would've moved on by now.

She bit the inside of her lip. Why *hadn't* she moved on by now?

"Tell me who's been offering lately." Rob leaned forward and rested his elbows on his knees, tenting his fingers.

"My neighbor, Amos Johnson, for one. Then there's Stanley Fitz, the senator? He's been pressuring me for years. Plus a whole slew of drilling companies interested in mineral rights."

Rob's eyebrows went up. "Really?"

She shifted in her seat, suddenly wondering if it was wise to spill this information to someone involved in realty.

At her momentary hesitation, Jesse said, "Apparently Dale Madsen learned the estate is unified, but then maybe you knew that?"

His uncle cocked his head. "What do you know about Senator Fitz? Have you ever had any contact with him?"

Sadie shook her head. "He's mainly communicated by mail, but he did have a realtor call me once or twice to make an offer over the phone. Said he loved my land and wanted to build a ranch in the Hole for his kids to enjoy."

What would it be like to have that much money? Where if you wanted something, you could just make offers until you got it? Fitz didn't have to pore over his accounting books every night trying to make ends meet.

Rob nodded. "I'll shoot straight with you. I've known Stanley for years—not well, but we've moved in the same circles. He's a very determined man once he sets his sights on something. And my personal hunch is he'd be more likely to recruit muscle from Casper than your neighbor. Amos lives next door—he could find plenty of ways to mess with your fences and cattle without resorting to hiring thugs from across the state."

"But why?" Jesse ran a hand through his hair. "Wouldn't the risk be too great? He's trying to win a seat in the federal senate in the next election. Surely, he wouldn't jeopardize his career over land for his kids." He flung an arm toward the windows. "Especially when there's plenty of other real estate here for sale."

"Well, if it's not him or Amos, then who is it?" Frustration bubbled inside Sadie's chest. Why did this need to be so difficult? And why did the Double M have to be the target? "Jesse, it's at least worth looking into Fitz further."

"Absolutely. We need to explore all the options." His calm tone made the bubbles expand beneath her ribs. "Uncle Rob, can you think of anyone else who might want the Double M?"

The older man's mouth twisted into a frown, and after a moment, he shook his head. "There's just not enough here to go on. But I think it's worthwhile to look into Senator Fitz, don't you? Like I said, he's not the type to back down once he's set his sights on something. I've spoken with his personal assistant before. Would you like me to see if we can set up a meeting? He's not going to pull anything suspicious. The political risks would be too great."

Regardless of what Rob said, would it be safe? Sadie glanced at Jesse to find his thoughtful blue gaze already on her. He dipped his chin in an almost imperceptible nod.

She released a slow breath through closed lips. They needed to do *something*, not just keep reacting, and this was the best lead they had. "All right. He's about an hour south, right?"

"Unless they're in session in Cheyenne." Rob reached for his cell phone. "Otherwise his home is just outside the Hole, near Pinedale." He tapped on his phone, then held it up to his ear. After a short conversation, he hung up. "Fitz can meet with you this afternoon at 4:00 p.m. at his home office. I'm texting Jesse the address for his ranch. You could also notify the police about the meeting if it makes you feel safer."

"Thanks." She bit her lip. Maybe she'd discuss that option with Jesse. "What about Kip?"

"You can leave him here, if you'd like," Rob offered.

Yet again she imagined Kip's nails digging into the flooring and furniture.

"He'll be fine coming along. We won't be there long," Jesse said, then rose to his feet. "It's after two. We should get going. I'd like time to scope out the area."

Sadie stood and walked with him to the door, then paused. "Rob, I know you and my father were close once. Do you happen to know if there were any charities around here he particularly wanted to support?"

It might be easier to come right out and ask if he knew about the named beneficiaries of her family trust, but why would her father have ever discussed it with Rob? Yes, they'd been friends, but would they have discussed their wills? She'd mentioned to Katrina that the ranch was part of a legacy trust, but only because it had come up when she was processing the aftermath of her parents' deaths.

Rob pursed his lips. "Hmm, nothing specific is coming to mind. I'll let you know if I come up with anything. Stay safe, and please tell me if you learn anything from Fitz."

She and Jesse shook hands with him at the door, then headed back to Jesse's truck. Kip barked from inside, and she smiled at the familiar sound. No matter how awful life got, there was nothing like the greeting of her dog to warm her insides. After letting him out to stretch his legs and get a drink, Jesse loaded the collie back into the truck.

As they drove toward the main road that would lead them south out of the Hole, Jesse glanced at her. "What do you think about this? You okay with going to see Fitz?"

She nodded, swallowing down her hesitation. "I think we need to. The police haven't been able to trace anything to him, but if your uncle thinks he's worth checking out, then it's a good idea."

"I'd like to poke around town, too, maybe see if there are any rumors about him, but we'll probably have to do that after the meeting."

"I'll text Deputy Freeman to let him know where we're going." She pulled out her phone and shot off a quick message, then let out a slow breath. At least the police would know where they were if anything *did* happen.

And maybe, just maybe, they'd learn something that would help bring this nightmare to an end.

The gate for Fitz's ranch—one of the largest private estates in Wyoming—loomed ahead in all its quarried stone and polished wood glory. Did he have workmen whose sole job was to keep that gate looking brand-new?

Jesse glanced at Sadie, resisting the urge to take one of her hands into his own. She'd been picking at her nails since they cleared the mountain pass out of the Hole, a sure indicator she was nervous.

"If this gate is locked, how are we going to leave?" she asked, sucking in a sharp breath.

He pulled up to the security box but turned to her first. "Sadie, he's not going to try something while we're here.

Not only did you tell the police about the meeting, but he'd never risk that kind of scandal."

She exhaled slowly. "I hope you're right."

After opening his window, Jesse pushed the red call button, and a moment later the big iron gates swung open. The paved road from the gate stretched across rolling grassland until they reached twin lines of huge bur oaks, decades old from the size of them. He gaped out the windshield, and Sadie's jaw fell open as the house—more like a ten-thousand-square-foot mansion—came into view. Built of stone and what appeared to be redwood, it was situated between a small lake on one side, a circle drive on the other and groves of evergreens behind. Quaking aspen, large rocks and terraced landings with Adirondack chairs completed the look of an idyllic Western resort.

"No wonder he could offer me cash," Sadie said breathlessly.

That meant he had plenty of cash to hire thugs, too. But why would anyone this rich want to do something so foolish, when it would put his career and future in jeopardy? Despite what Rob had hinted, the math didn't add up. Or was he just inclined to disagree with anything Rob suggested?

Jesse pulled the truck to a stop in the drive, and Sadie cracked the windows for Kip, who was sleeping on the back seat. They'd barely gotten their doors open when he noticed a security guard speaking into a walkie-talkie near the lower level of the house. The man pulled open a glass door, and a woman dressed in a tailored suit came out, heading their direction.

"You must be Ranger Taylor and Ms. Madsen," she said as she approached, then shook hands with each of them.

"Mr. Fitz is wrapping up his three o'clock, but if you'll come this way, I can get you something to drink while you're waiting."

They followed her inside to a sitting area that boasted a view of the distant mountains and overlooked thousands of acres of roaming cattle. Were all those Fitz's animals? Or did he rent out grazing land? Regardless, he probably had a manager in charge of all his business ventures.

The woman, who had introduced herself as Heidi, Fitz's personal assistant, offered them cold bottles of water from a mini fridge built into a small kitchenette and then left to check on the senator.

Sadie paced back and forth as they waited, twisting the bottle in her hands. Her long braid swung around her shoulders each time she reached the end of the room and turned.

"Sadie?" Jesse patted the seat next to him. "You're going to wear a hole in Fitz's carpet."

She paused long enough to offer him a scowl. "He can afford to replace it."

Heidi appeared in the doorway. "Senator Fitz is ready to see you now."

He and Sadie followed her down a plush carpeted hallway. Sadie kept glancing around, checking over her shoulder and surveying closed doors they passed, so he rested a hand against her back and leaned closer. "We're going to be fine."

"Just because everything looks professional doesn't mean he's not up to something," she shot back in a whisper.

Heidi stopped in front of a large six-panel door made of dark, glossy wood. She tapped gently, then opened it when a man's voice said, "Come on in."

Stanley Fitz rose from behind his desk and walked

around it to greet them. Dressed in a plaid shirt and dark blue jeans, he looked right at home with the panoramic view of the mountains in the picture window behind him. A silver Rolex glinted at his wrist as he shook Jesse's hand, and the bookshelves of the office were lined with works of art and framed cases of rare coins.

Despite the display of wealth, the man himself came across as friendly enough as he offered them seats and then leaned against his desk, crossing one ankle over the other.

"Now, Ms. Madsen, Mr. Taylor, what can I do for you? Your uncle, I believe—Rob Clark—told my assistant it had to do with the Double M Ranch. Are you interested in working out a deal?"

Sadie darted a glance at Jesse, her eyebrows folding into a scowl. But just because the man still wanted to buy her property didn't make him a villain. Not automatically, anyway.

"We do have some questions related to the ranch," Jesse said slowly, pulling his gaze away from her and turning back to Fitz. "Have the police been in touch with you?"

Fitz folded his arms across his chest, and his mouth opened as understanding passed across his features. "*That's* why the Teton County Sheriff's Department requested a phone interview. Heidi scheduled it for me tomorrow morning. Does this have something to do with the ranch?" He angled his head to one side.

Was the man playing dumb, or was he innocent? Jesse's gut said the latter, but from the way Sadie was shooting daggers his direction, she didn't agree. He opened his mouth to ask if she wanted to answer Fitz, but she gave a nearly imperceptible shake of her head.

"Yes, actually, it does," he said, watching Fitz carefully

for a reaction. "There have been a number of incidents at the ranch, escalating to personal attacks on Sadie."

Fitz's brows pulled together. "I'm so sorry to hear this, Ms. Madsen."

She gave him a tight nod.

"The police have traced the attacks to three men from the Casper area," he continued. "As there's no known connection between these men and Sadie or the Double M, we believe they were hired by someone else with the intention of threatening her into selling."

"Oh, that's terrible," the senator said. "But if I may ask, what does this have to do with me?" He unfolded his arms and braced them against the desk, leaning forward. Genuinely confused? Or daring them to make an accusation, perhaps.

"We're hoping to explore every possible angle for who might be behind these attacks," Jesse said, choosing to go with tact over brute force. If the senator was innocent, he didn't want to lose his goodwill. "The police have one of the men in custody, but they haven't been able to question him yet."

Sadie shifted in her seat, leaning toward Fitz. "Exactly how badly do you want my ranch, Senator Fitz?"

Jesse cleared his throat. Loudly. "I'm sorry, Senator, I'm sure Sadie didn't mean for that to come across so—"

Fitz held up a hand, then stroked his clean-shaven chin as his lips turned up. He couldn't have been more than a decade older than Jesse, late thirties or early forties. "No, it's okay. Ms. Madsen has been under a lot of stress lately, from what you've told me. I'm sorry that my offers have come across so aggressively that you'd think I might be involved. But please let me assure you, as much as I love your particular patch of land, I'd never harm someone to try to get it."

Her mouth pursed in a classic-Sadie *I don't believe you* expression, but she kept her thoughts to herself.

"Can you think of anyone who might?" Jesse asked. "Have you ever run across someone else who seemed interested in her land?"

Fitz shook his head. "No, I haven't. I can ask my realtor, though, if that would help. She might have heard something."

"Thank you, we'd appreciate it." Now that Fitz appeared to be a dead end, it was probably best to get Sadie out of here before she said anything else accusatory. Maybe they'd find some leads in Pinedale after asking around. "Well, thank you for taking the time to meet with us." Jesse rose to his feet and extended his hand to Fitz.

"Of course," Fitz said, shaking it before turning to Sadie. "If there's anything else I can do, please let me know. And while my offer for the ranch still stands, I won't send further letters or intrude on you in any way."

"Thank you," she replied. Fitz probably didn't notice, but her tone was decidedly brittle. She stuffed both hands in her pockets before he could offer to shake with her.

By the time Heidi escorted them back outside, the innocent clouds from earlier had developed into thick, dark storm clouds blanketing the peaks in the west. The wind was picking up, blowing dust into phantom snakes slithering across the driveway.

"Looks like rain." Jesse hustled to the truck and unlocked the doors. They'd left the windows down for Kip— good thing the meeting hadn't lasted longer.

"Well, that was a waste," Sadie huffed as she buckled

her seat belt. "Obviously he wasn't going to come right out and admit what he's been doing."

Jesse braced both hands on the wheel and turned to look at her. "Really? You *still* think he's the one behind all of this?"

"I—" She slammed her mouth shut, cheeks turning pink. "If it's not Stanley Fitz, then who is it? Even your uncle thinks he's the most likely culprit."

Just because Uncle Rob thought something didn't mean he was right.

He put the truck into Drive, circled around the front loop, and headed for the entrance gate. "Let's go into Pinedale, get some dinner, and poke around. Maybe we'll hear something. And then tomorrow we'll look into other options, like your neighbor. And that charity named as beneficiary of the trust."

She tugged out her cell phone as he turned east onto the highway. "Still no message from Mike. I've got a meeting with him tomorrow afternoon, so I'll find out then."

Ten minutes later, they pulled up in front of a local diner in Pinedale. Thunder rumbled in the distance, making Kip shift restlessly on the back seat.

"It's fixin' to pour," Sadie said, watching lightning crackle across the sky in the west. She grabbed Kip's leash. "I'm going to let Kip out for a few minutes before the rain gets here. We won't be able to leave him in the car for long, not with the thunder."

Jesse nodded. "I'll run in and place a to-go order and see what I can learn. Stay close, okay? And scream if anyone tries anything."

Her lips curled into a faint smile. "I won't let anyone kidnap me. Besides, Kip will protect me."

Jesse had gotten so used to that job over the past several days, it was hard to think about the fact that he'd be walking back out of her life soon. Yet he'd have to accept the idea, because Sadie didn't want him, and he couldn't risk letting her down again. No, things were better this way.

He tugged open the door to the diner and found a menu at the counter, realizing he'd forgotten to ask Sadie what she wanted. In the old days it would've been a BLT with extra bacon and a side of fries. Did she still eat the same things? It struck him all at once how badly he wanted to know, and not just her meal habits, but everything about her. Did she still like the same music? Did she ever go line dancing anymore?

Had she dated anyone since him?

"What can I get you, hon?" An older woman in her sixties, her hair pulled back in a short ponytail, stood in front of him with a pen and notepad.

"Uh…" He'd been so lost in his thoughts he hadn't even looked at the menu. Oh well, he was going to guess for Sadie anyway. He rattled off the same order he would've placed ten years ago plus a plain grilled chicken sandwich for Kip, then waited as the waitress attached their order to a clip and spun it around for the line cook. "Is that Senator Fitz's ranch just to the west of here?" he asked, trying to sound casual.

"The big place with the fancy gate? Yessir. Nice, ain't it?"

He let out a low whistle. "Been in the family a long time, or did he buy it?"

"One Fitz or another has owned that place my entire life. Always been rich, so far as I know. Not like us normal folk. But then I'd never be cut out for politics, neither."

As he'd suspected, Fitz hadn't come into sudden money. Why would he jeopardize everything over Sadie's land? The motive just wasn't there. Uncle Rob had seemed to think otherwise, but why? Maybe tomorrow while Sadie met with her financial advisor, he'd talk to Rob again. Without Sadie there, maybe his uncle would be more willing to confide his suspicions. He shot off a few quick texts to his uncle, setting a time to meet at his place.

By the time he walked out with their food, the sky had darkened, and the first drops of rain pinged off the roof of the truck. His chest tightened as he looked for Sadie, then relaxed as she and Kip came jogging from around the side of the diner's parking lot.

"Oh, good, you're back," she panted as they ran up to him. Kip's long pink tongue lolled out on one side.

"Any sign of trouble?" he asked, glancing past her around the lot.

"Just the weather." She nodded toward the storm clouds blotting out the early evening daylight. "Did you learn anything?"

He unlocked the truck, placed their drinks inside and handed her the bag of hot food. After helping Kip inside, he climbed in behind the wheel. The rain was still falling as an innocent sprinkle, but it wouldn't be long before they'd be in a deluge. "Just that the Fitz family has owned that land for decades. I can't figure out for the life of me why he'd risk everything to threaten you."

"Maybe he's confident he won't get caught," she said, but her tone lacked the conviction it held earlier. She rubbed her forehead, carefully avoiding the greenish-yellow spot where the bruise was still healing. "I don't know, maybe it's a dead end. If you're okay with driving in the rain, maybe we should get going. It's a long haul back to the ranch."

"Fine with me." He turned on the engine and backed the truck out of the parking spot, then pointed to the bag. "I had to guess what you'd want. And I got something for Kip."

"That was thoughtful of you." The paper crinkled as she opened the sack, then rummaged inside. She laughed as she peeked into the packages. "Can't go wrong with a good BLT. And the bacon cheeseburger is for you, right?"

"Just like the old days." The words slipped out before he could catch them. Would she wince? Pull away from him and grow stony cold?

Instead, she lifted her paper cup of root beer and held it up in a mock toast. "To the old days."

He picked his up and tapped it against hers.

"We had some good times together, didn't we?" She said the words almost wistfully, then took a long sip of soda. "Thanks for helping me, Jesse. I know I've said it a few times already, but I hope you know how much I mean it. I don't know what I'd do without you right now."

The space under his ribs filled with warmth. In all honesty she'd probably do just fine without him—someone else would've stepped up and helped her. But he was so grateful it hadn't worked out that way. "God put me in the right place at the right time."

"He sure did." She popped a French fry into her mouth as she handed him his cheeseburger, then gave Kip the chicken sandwich.

Eating while driving wasn't his favorite, but he managed to avoid dripping ketchup on his lap as he downed the hot food. Next to him, Sadie sighed, a small smile playing at her mouth as she ate her sandwich. Apparently her love for bacon hadn't faded with time.

As they turned onto the highway and left Pinedale behind, giant drops of rain splattered against the windshield in isolated *plops*. Up ahead, he could see the gray mist obscuring the road as they approached the heavier rainfall. "Here it comes."

Within seconds the truck hit a veritable wall of rain, pummeling the windshield so hard, Jesse could barely see. He tapped the brakes and glanced at the speedometer, then did a double take. Why was the engine running so hot?

"Sadie…" The pounding rain filled his ears and obscured his vision, but now that he was paying attention, he could almost smell a faint odor of something burning. His engine? He grimaced, slowing down more.

"Do you need to pull off?" she called over the din of the rain. Thunder crackled, and a bolt of lightning lit up the darkening sky.

"I'm gonna have to—look at the engine temperature."

She leaned against him, stretching to see the gauge in the lower right corner. Her face twisted into a frown. "Coolant leak?"

He flipped on his hazard flashers just in case anyone else was out here. "We're close to Fitz's ranch. I'll turn in there."

"Isn't that convenient?" Her tone dripped sarcasm. "When's the last time you checked the fluids?"

"Two months? Right before I moved out here." He shook his head. "Doesn't matter right now. We have to stop, regardless. Even if I can fix it myself, we'll need a ride back into town to buy more antifreeze and parts."

When they reached Fitz's ranch, he turned into the driveway and got drenched talking to security. But the gates rolled open, and he steered the truck slowly back toward the house.

Sadie sat stiff as a statue next to him, the container of fries growing cold in her lap, probably thinking the same unspoken questions. Was the coolant leak a coincidence, or had someone tampered with his truck?

And more pressing, had they done it on Stanley Fitz's orders?

NINE

Jesse dashed around the back of the truck in the pummeling rain as Sadie clipped Kip's leash onto his collar and helped him down. As they ran for the house, the hail started, pelting their faces and heads with sharp little chunks of ice.

They stopped inside the door, shaking off water and catching their breath, then Jesse explained to the security guard what had happened. A crease formed between Sadie's brows. She hadn't been too thrilled coming back here, but he didn't see another alternative. Not with this storm.

Mighty convenient, though, how they'd run out of coolant right in front of Fitz's ranch. Was there something to his uncle's suspicions after all?

Heidi, Fitz's personal assistant, appeared a minute later. "Ms. Madsen, Mr. Taylor, I'm so sorry to hear about the car trouble. The senator wanted to me to convey his sympathies and let you know you're welcome to stay here overnight. The ranch has several guest rooms. Your dog is welcome, too." Kip wagged his tail when Heidi smiled at him.

Jesse glanced at his watch. The auto parts stores would all be closed in Pinedale by now. Maybe they'd be able to get lodging in town, but they'd still need a ride. The senator would know their exact location—*if* he'd orchestrated this plan. Jesse still had his doubts, but the scowl on Sadie's face spoke volumes about her opinion.

Still, he wasn't going to ask her to stay somewhere she wasn't comfortable, especially not after everything she'd endured. Her brown eyes met his, and he raised his brows, letting her know it was her call.

She turned to Heidi. "We'd be very grateful for a place to stay. Please thank Senator Fitz for us. And is there somewhere to throw this away?" She held out their trash from dinner.

"Of course." The other woman vanished with the wet sack.

He left Sadie inside as he dashed back out to grab the overnight bags he'd insisted they pack. If there was one thing he'd learned as a park ranger, it was that preparation was key. And with the way things had been going, it didn't hurt to have your own toothbrush on hand.

They followed Heidi up a flight of stairs and down one wing of the house, where she showed them to side-by-side guest rooms. "There's a sitting area with a kitchenette down the hall. Please help yourself to tea or coffee. Senator Fitz's family occupies the opposite wing, so you'll have your privacy here. If you need anything, dial one on the phone in the kitchenette, or you can text my number."

Sadie shot him a glance. Just like staying at a bed-and-breakfast. Or a luxury resort.

After thanking Heidi, he waited in the doorway of Sadie's room as she went in. Kip wandered in first, sniffing everything he passed.

A large picture window overlooked the ranch's property. The house had been built into the landscape so that their rooms were on the ground floor on this side, even though they'd come up a flight of steps from the lower level. The furniture was rustic but well made, and the whole place gave off an air of tasteful luxury.

He whistled. "Nice in here. I wonder how many guests the man has?"

"I know." She said it softly, almost wistfully. "And how many rooms in this wing sit unused regularly?"

He threw a thumb toward his room. "I'm going to get dried off. Meet me down in the kitchenette in thirty minutes? We can go over our next steps."

"Sure. I'd love a cup of tea before bed."

Jesse brewed himself a cup of decaf and had the electric kettle humming when Sadie appeared in the sitting room half an hour later. He held out a mug as she approached the counter. "Thanks." She scanned a rack of tea boxes, choosing one of the bags.

When they'd both settled into chairs, he set his mug on the coffee table. "After what happened this evening," he said, keeping his voice low, "we probably shouldn't write Fitz off yet. But I still don't see what he's going to gain by hunting you down. The charity is the only one I can think of who would benefit from…" He let the awful thought trail away as he cracked his knuckles. Who could want Sadie's land badly enough to harm her? "Though I don't know how Dale would've chosen any nonprofit that mercenary."

Sadie rubbed her eyes. She had to be exhausted. "Me, neither. Whatever organization he picked, he probably never expected they'd receive anything. He and Mom were far too young."

Something twisted painfully in his chest. "I'm sorry, Sadie." Before he could think better of it, he reached out and took her hand, squeezing gently before releasing. "I should have been there for you."

Even with all his shortcomings, she'd needed him, and he hadn't been there. She'd had to face all that loss and pain alone. Grief sucked the air from his chest, made worse by the way her dark brown eyes had gone liquid.

She sucked in a ragged breath. "Thanks, Jesse. I wish you had been."

Did she mean that? If they could go back, would she still choose him, even though she knew what mistakes he was capable of making?

For a moment, as their gazes connected, the past seemed to vanish. All he could think about was how she'd grown even more beautiful over the years, inside and out. She'd extended an olive branch to him these past few days, confiding in him, trusting him. That simple act of faith tied his insides into knots.

A faint blush tinted her cheeks, and her throat bobbed. She looked down at the mug in her hands. Warmth crept up the back of his neck as he realized he'd been staring into her eyes, and he forced his attention back to his coffee.

She cleared her throat. "I'm planning on getting the charity's information from Mike during our meeting tomorrow. What about the drilling companies who've contacted me? I know the police haven't turned anything up with them yet, but what if—"

Both their phones pinged, and he glanced down to read the text. "Deputy Freeman," he said. "Barts won't talk without a lawyer."

"I got the same message," she said.

He checked his other notifications. "There's a text from the chief ranger, too. They found the weapon the other man dropped—purchased by Gordon Davis in a store in Casper. But the man has eluded capture so far."

"More dead ends." She wrapped her arms across her chest. The look of exhaustion on her face made him want to wrap her up in a warm embrace.

Out of the question. "I'll get outside to look at the truck first thing in the morning. Your meeting with the financial advisor is at three o'clock tomorrow, right?"

"Yes. I hope he has answers." She took a sip of her tea, and the air filled with the calming scent of mint. "Either that or we bide our time, waiting for the police to finish their interviews. The drilling companies. Amos. The geologist who examined my land." Sadie stood and carried her mug to the sink.

"Let me take Kip out for you," he offered, rising also, "and then get some sleep, okay? It's been a long day."

They walked down the hall to their rooms, and she brought Kip out on his leash. Jesse took him back to the sitting room, which had a sliding door leading outside. By the time he brought the collie back a few minutes later, Sadie looked ready to crash.

He waited until she'd closed and locked her door, then returned to his own room, where he tossed and turned as sleep evaded him. Not only was Sadie's life at risk, but he was growing more certain by the hour that his heart was at risk, too. Being this close to her and not feeling anything for her was impossible. They needed to figure out who was behind these attacks once and for all, before it was too late.

Sadie crawled wearily under the covers as Kip settled onto a blanket near the side of the bed. This day had dragged on for an eternity. And Jesse... He'd been her rock—always there for her, considerate, self-sacrificing. Between that and the way his gorgeous blue eyes had studied her earlier... Well, it was high time to go to sleep and stop thinking about him.

She felt as if she'd barely closed her eyes when a crash jolted her awake, as if something had fallen off a shelf. But was it real or part of a dream? Sleep dragged at her brain, trying to pull her back into its delicious warmth.

Somewhere nearby Kip barked.

"Kip, knock it off," she muttered, fumbling for a pillow to put over her head. Where was she, anyway?

Kip's low growl rattled her out of her haze of slumber.

Fitz's ranch—that was where she was. She pried the pillow off her head just in time to feel a cold metal ring press into her back.

"Tell the dog to shut up, now," a low voice ordered. "And keep him back, or I'll shoot."

Every hair on her arms stood up as a chill raked her skin. "Quiet, Kip," she said, though the dog kept growling. Her voice trembled. "Stay."

The room was too dark to see if the collie had obeyed. She didn't doubt for a minute this man would hurt Kip if he attacked. What was riskier, to fight back or let him take her? She couldn't let him hurt Kip.

Then a damp rag clamped over her mouth, filled with some awful, sweet, chemical smell that made everything spin. Her limbs turned into useless lumps attached to her body, her brain a pile of pudding. The world tilted, and everything went black.

Fresh air, heavy with the scent of rain, wafted across her face and scattered her hair across her forehead. The heavy, dull feeling in her head started to recede as someone dropped her into the back seat of a vehicle. Her cheek pressed against cold leather, and her knees crunched up near her chest to fit in the tight space.

She struggled to push herself up, but her arms were limp as wilted lettuce. The best she could manage was forcing her heavy eyelids open to stare at the dashboard lights. A man climbed into the passenger seat, then pulled his door shut.

"Go, now!" he barked, slapping his hand on the dash. "That stupid mutt is going to wake up the entire house. We gotta get outta here."

She knew that voice—it was the burly guy, Davis. The one who'd gotten away from Jesse up on the mountain. He must've escaped the other rangers, too. Was the driver the same too? Warden?

The vehicle lurched, sending her sliding into the seatback.

"We'll get away from the house a bit, then take care of her," Warden said. Dread coiled in her stomach. Were they going to kill her right now?

"No way. We don't have time for that now," Davis argued. "Get away first, do the job later."

Adrenaline fired through her system, tripling her heart rate and making it hard to breathe, but she forced herself to take a slow breath. Panicking wouldn't help. As whatever they'd drugged her with wore off, she could feel the strength returning to her muscles, her mind working more clearly. The SUV wasn't moving very fast, and from the way it bounced over rough terrain, she guessed they hadn't left Fitz's property yet.

"What happened to your brain cells, Davis?" the driver snapped. "Boss says we have to do it here. How else are we gonna make it look like it's the senator's fault?"

Her eyes widened. They were going to frame Fitz for her murder. Jesse had been right—the senator wasn't involved. Then who was their boss?

She wasn't going to linger around here to find out. Quietly, so they wouldn't know she was alert, she tested her hands and feet for movement. Everything felt back to normal. As her eyes adjusted to the darkness, she scanned the inside of the vehicle. It appeared to be an old SUV—maybe the green Bronco that had been at the trailhead.

Panic tightened its noose around her neck. That old Bronco only had two doors. She'd have no way to jump out. Unless...

Maybe she could get out the rear hatch window, over the tailgate. Judging by the interior, this vehicle was old enough it didn't have power locks. If she could get over the seat back and out the window quick enough, maybe she could catch them off guard,

She rolled onto her back, moving as quietly as she could. The SUV's loud clattering as it jostled over the dirt road helped conceal the sound.

"What's that noise?" Davis asked.

She froze, holding her breath.

"It's an engine," he said. "Somebody's coming. Go faster!"

"I can't see a blasted thing in this fog," Warden snapped. "We gotta pull over into one of these fields and just do it. Then we can go."

"No way, man. I didn't survive that night in the wild just to get caught now. Go!" Davis urged.

Her eyes slammed shut as the driver pivoted in his seat, turning to look at her. "You got your gun. Just do it now and we'll dump the body real quick."

All the hairs shot up on her arms as her skin prickled

with goose bumps. Should she dive to the floor? Try to get over the seatback?

"Whoa, watch out!" Davis shouted.

The driver slammed the brakes, sending Sadie sliding forward on the seat. She had to make her move now, while they were distracted.

Rolling over, she grabbed for the top of the seatback. As soon as her hands connected with the curved leather of a headrest, she hoisted herself up and tumbled headfirst into the back of the Bronco.

Davis and Warden were yelling in the front as the Bronco rumbled over a cattle guard, but she didn't linger to listen to the commotion. When her scrabbling fingers found the metal latch to the liftgate, she twisted and shoved the window open, then flung herself out of the vehicle.

A twin pair of oncoming headlights blinded her, but the ground was coming fast and hard. Her hands hit first, biting into rough gravel, and she managed to tuck into a roll on her shoulder instead of face-planting.

She rolled to a stop in the middle of the road. An approaching ATV slammed to a halt, leaving her blinking in a puddle of light.

"Sadie!" Jesse called, and relief flooded her insides. "Stay down," he ordered. The sharp crack of a gun split the night, shattering one of the Bronco's taillights.

The passenger door, which had started to open, pulled shut and the engine roared to life as the Bronco took off.

Footsteps pounded across the dirt as Jesse ran up to her. He knelt, scanning her from head to toe. "Sadie, are you all right?"

She pushed herself into a sitting position. "I think so.

Nothing seems broken. But I feel kind of like a bruised peach."

He cupped a hand beneath her chin, turning her head gently as he examined her eye tracking. "That was quite a tumble you just took. Come here."

After helping her to her feet, he caught her up in his arms. She pressed her face into the space between his shoulder and neck, warm and secure, breathing in his comforting scent.

Her entire body ached, but her insides merely felt numb. How many more times could she come this close to death and still survive? And Jesse, and even Kip—they were constantly in danger, too. All because of a piece of land. Was this God's way of telling her to stop being so stubborn?

"Come on, let's get you back." Jesse released her but kept an arm around her as they walked back to the ATV. As much as she hated to admit it to herself, she needed his strength right now.

"What happened?" he asked.

"Somebody broke into my room. He had a gun and a rag soaked in some chemical that knocked me out. When I came to, I was in the back of their vehicle."

He helped her onto the ATV, then slid onto the seat in front of her. "Was it both of them? Warden and that other man from the trail, Davis?"

"Yes." She related the details of her escape as he fired up the ATV and turned it around. "It's a good thing you showed up when you did." A shudder rippled through her spine.

"We have Kip to thank for waking me up," Jesse said. "And the Lord for protecting you."

"Amen to that." She offered up her own silent prayer of gratitude. The Lord had seen fit to keep her on this earth a little longer, but what was she going to do with that gift? Keep putting herself in danger, so Jesse had to keep upending his life to protect hers? How was that fair to him?

"Had to borrow this since my truck is out of commission." He patted the ATV's handlebars. "Cops are on the way, too. And hopefully Kip has woken up the entire household by now." His back went rigid. "It's time for another word with Stanley Fitz."

"Jesse… I don't think it was him." She let out a long sigh. "I overheard them arguing. The one who abducted me—the bigger guy, Davis—wanted to get away before Kip woke somebody up and they were caught. But Warden insisted their boss wanted them to kill—" she paused as Jesse flinched "—do it here and leave my body on the ranch. It was supposed to be a setup to make Fitz look guilty."

"And remove you as owner of the Double M. But the only party who really benefits from you being out of the picture is—"

"The charity," she finished for him. "Or possibly one of the drilling companies, though I don't see how. I need to talk to Mike. And then…" She forced out the words she'd been avoiding for far too long. "It's time to sell the ranch."

No matter how much that idea hurt, she had to find a way to move on. She'd gotten over Jesse, and she'd get over this, too. Anything would be better than living in this constant state of danger and uncertainty. Even giving up her dream.

TEN

Jesse felt like she'd scalded him with a hot iron. "What?"

"I can't keep doing this, Jesse." Her voice trembled as she spoke, tugging at all the tender places inside that cared about her so much. "Living life in fear. Putting you in danger. You have your own life. You shouldn't have to keep spending it taking care of me."

But what if that's how I want *to spend it?*

The words flashed through his brain at light speed, so far out of left field he let the question shoot right on past. Sadie wasn't thinking anything along those lines—in fact, what she was saying communicated exactly the opposite: I'm ready for you to be out of my life, even if it means selling my beloved ranch. His heart needed to get the memo. Letting her in again was a surefire path to more hurt. Sure, there was a dull ache below his ribs right now, but why make it worse?

Sadie was stubborn to a fault—if she'd made up her mind, there was little he'd be able to say to talk her out of it. That went for both the ranch and for the idea of him sticking around to help her, in any capacity. They hadn't even investigated the charity yet. Maybe it was the lead they were looking for. But would Sadie be willing to wait until tomorrow afternoon? He doubted it.

"Well, you still have time to think about it," he managed to choke out past the lump forming in his throat.

Day was breaking in the east by the time they pulled up in front of Fitz's estate again. A police car sat parked out front. The officer, a couple of security guards, and Stanley Fitz stood nearby. After Jesse shut off the engine and they climbed down, Kip came dashing up to her, barking happily.

The worried look on Fitz's face corroborated what Sadie had overhead. He draped a blanket over her shoulders, and they all walked inside. After they'd given their statements, Jesse left her with Heidi and went out to inspect his truck. The fact she was even willing to sit inside Fitz's house without him spoke volumes.

A quick inspection of the engine revealed that one of the radiator hoses had been slit, allowing the coolant to slowly leak out. He showed the damage to the police officer, who took some photographs and asked a few questions.

The damage definitely looked intentional rather than accidental, and the timing matched perfectly. Whoever had sent those men for Sadie had known where to find them and had done their best to make sure she'd be here overnight. A shiver tracked across Jesse's shoulders. Whoever they were up against wasn't messing around.

Even worse, the police called to notify him and Sadie that they'd found the Bronco abandoned at a nearby gas station. It had been stolen in Jackson a few days prior. There was no sign of the men. The police suspected they'd escaped undetected in the back of pickup or tractor trailer stopping for gas.

By early afternoon, Fitz had helped arrange for Jesse to get a new hose, install it and refill the radiator with coolant. He apologized again to Jesse and Sadie, inviting them to stay at the ranch anytime they were back in the area.

The way Sadie's shoulders slumped as she carried her bag out to the truck made his heart hurt.

"Did you say anything to Fitz?" he asked as they drove up the highway toward Jackson Hole. "About selling?"

She played with the end of her long braid. "Not yet. I need to discuss it with Mike first. Jackson Financial has to sign off as cotrustee, but there's no reason for the bank not to if Fitz is giving us a fair price."

"Sadie…"

She twisted in her seat, staring out the side window. Like she wanted to avoid talking about it.

What did he want to say, anyway? *I care about you? I don't want you to give up on your dream? My feelings for you haven't changed, even after all these years?*

How many times had he wanted to talk to her and say words like those in the months after he'd left? During those lonely days up in Denali, his first NPS assignment, when he'd had few distractions from his heartache and fewer friends, he'd come *this* close to spilling the truth when she'd called. The pain in her tone had crushed his already fractured heart.

But going back to face everything he'd run from, to face Dale and his uncle again, and Sadie and what he'd done to her… He couldn't do it. *You could reach great heights, kid, if you just made better choices.* Even after all these years, Uncle Rob's voice *still* played in his head.

What he hated most of all was that Rob had been right.

He swallowed hard and let the silence in the car settle

over them. These feelings would go away eventually. Or
at least they'd go dormant, as they had for so many years.

As they approached town, gas stations and oil change
places and pharmacies flashed past. Too soon, he pulled
into a spot in the Jackson Financial parking lot, leaving
the truck idling. They'd already agreed he would keep Kip
with him until she called when the appointment was over.

"Looks like you'll be right on time," he said woodenly.
"What will you do? If you don't have the ranch?"

She blinked a few times. "I'll find something. I always
land on my feet. God helps those who help themselves,
right?"

When she glanced at him, the pain in her dark eyes
burned his insides. If he hadn't left her all those years ago,
everything would be different right now. He could have
spared her so much hurt.

The weight of shame and guilt pressed down on his
shoulders like a hundred-pound bag of animal feed.
"Sadie… God helps those who put their trust in Him. He
can do anything He wants. Without *our* help. I know you've
been through a lot, with your parents and keeping the ranch
afloat. I'm sorry for leaving you to pick up the pieces alone."

Her throat bobbed, and she looked out the window instead of meeting his gaze. "I never knew anyone's heart
could hurt that badly." The words came out thick like por-
ridge, and they jabbed into his insides like a knife. But he
needed to hear. Needed to give her space to speak. "When
you left… I felt so blindsided, like I should've seen it coming, but I didn't. And then, Mom and Dad, and now the
ranch and these men… If God has a plan in it, I can't see
it. All I can figure is that I'm not doing enough. Or not the
right things. It's time to quit fighting."

He sucked his lower lip, trying to will away the burning in his eyes. "Sadie, I'm so sorry for hurting you. You don't know how much I wish I could undo all of it." So very much. The regret threatened to torch his insides, as if he'd drunk a bucket of lava. "But just because I left you alone doesn't mean God ever will. You don't have to earn His help or His love. I hope you know that."

When she finally turned to him, her eyes were glossy. She pressed her lips together and nodded. "I have to go," she said thickly, then opened the door and jumped from the truck. "I'll text when we're done."

The door slammed shut. Kip whined as the collie watched her walk away, his tail wagging in the back seat.

Jesse turned and scratched his back. "I know how you feel, boy." He faced the front again, then dragged a hand over his face. Why had he let Dale Madsen run him off all those years ago? And why had Dale been so opposed to Jesse in the first place?

He had insisted Jesse was wrong for Sadie. That she needed somebody who'd grown up on a ranch, not a "city boy" like Jesse, as he'd called him—hardly fair, considering Jesse *had* lived on a ranch until his father passed and Uncle Rob had taken him and his mom under his wing. He'd even gone so far as to accuse Jesse of dishonesty. His words still burned.

You don't really love my daughter. You just want what's in it for you, and you'll walk away as soon as you get the chance. So walk away now, before you crush her.

Well, he'd crushed her anyway. Even though he *had* really loved her. So much that he'd never recovered. The years apart had dulled the pain, but now it was back, hot and searing and fresh, like an old wound that had been reopened.

The funny thing was, he'd never been able to figure out what he'd done to make Dale distrust him. Sadie's parents had always liked him when they were teenagers. When they started dating, he'd get regular invitations to their home for meals.

Even after the rupture between his uncle and Sadie's father, Dale had still treated him well for months. Until that one day, when he'd pulled Jesse into his office "for a chat."

He'd always wondered what had happened to change Dale's mind, but Jesse could hardly call him up to ask after dumping his daughter practically at the altar. And, if he were being honest, it wasn't only Dale's opinion that had made him walk away—it was his own fear of not being enough for Sadie.

He'd let these questions go unexplored long enough, though. Now that he was back, maybe he could get some answers.

He had the meeting with his uncle soon, but first he reached for his phone and pulled up his mother's number. He'd never pressed her, but maybe she knew more than she'd told him. When she picked up, he gave her a brief update on Sadie's situation.

After reassuring her that Sadie was still safe, he asked, "Mom, what happened with Dale Madsen and Uncle Rob? What was their business arrangement that went south?"

A long sigh came through the phone. "I wish I knew, son. They went through a phase of regular arguing before Dale broke off all contact. Rob wouldn't talk about it." She paused. When she spoke again, the words were soft, almost hesitant. "I hate to say it, but I think that's why Dale didn't want you and Sadie together. I tried to ask Rob about it, but all he would say was that 'Dale knew what was best for his daughter.'"

Acid burned in the pit of Jesse's stomach. Had Uncle Rob gone back to Dale later and tried to break up Jesse and Sadie's engagement? And if so, why? Was Uncle Rob being so helpful now because he felt guilty about what had happened in the past? Clearly, he'd played *some* role in Dale's change of heart toward Jesse.

It was time to find out exactly what had happened between his uncle and Dale Madsen.

Sadie couldn't remember the last time she'd felt this fragile. Not even a few days ago in the hospital, when she'd had to confront Jesse for the first time right on the heels of her barn being torched.

No, this feeling was far worse. Maybe more like that day when Jesse had broken their engagement and left. She'd collapsed to her knees in a pile of hay in the barn and wept until she'd had no tears left to cry. Then she'd dried her face and finished her chores, because crying wasn't going to bring him back.

This time she skipped the tears and went straight to the emotionless aftermath. She just felt empty. Hollow. Like a rain barrel that had been drained dry and left to crack in the sun.

"Sadie?" Mike Schmidt's concerned gaze dragged her attention back across the desk, where he'd opened a manila file folder and was thumbing through a printed document. "You understand why we're hesitant to agree to sell, right?"

She bit her lip. Why did *everything* have to be hard? *Couldn't just this one thing be easy, Lord?* "Ultimately I think my father intended for me to make the decisions about the ranch," she said, trying to infuse her voice with strength she didn't feel.

Mike tented his fingers. "Yes and no. He clearly valued your judgment, but instead of making you sole trustee, he elected to make Jackson Financial a cotrustee with you. In doing so, he conferred on us the responsibility of making sure his wishes were followed."

"But my father never even mentioned this charity before," she spluttered. "What's it called? Children's United Way of Wyoming? Is that connected to the national United Way?"

After leafing through the papers in front of him, Mike handed her a sheet of paper. "Here, look at this. It's the instructions from your father when he established CUWW as the secondary beneficiary."

She took the page and stared at it. It was a formal typed letter, printed in Times New Roman. Dale Madsen's signature was at the bottom, though this paper looked like a copy rather than the original. He'd always been a straight-to-the-point type of person, and this letter was no different, briefly expressing his desire to name CUWW as beneficiary in hopes of benefiting children in the case that Sadie never had any of her own.

"Do you have the original?" she asked as she handed the sheet back to Mike.

He glanced up from his cell phone, almost as if startled, but then set it aside. "In our archives. It was scanned and attached to the electronic document. I printed this copy for your records."

"Thanks. I'll look into it."

"The, ah, address is close by if you'd like to visit for yourself." He shifted in his chair, then rubbed his shoulder as if it were stiff. "I haven't been there, but I recognize the street name."

"I will." She let out a sigh, then forced her sagging spine to straighten. "I understand your reasoning, but here's the thing. My father *did* name me cotrustee because he wanted me to have a say in what happens to the ranch. He would never have wanted my life in danger. And right now, that's exactly the way things are. I can't keep living like this."

Mike's brows pulled together as he nodded. "I'm so sorry you've had to go through this, Sadie. You're right, Dale would have hated to see you in this much danger. Let me see what we can do. I'll get in touch with Senator Fitz regarding his offer, and then I'll need to present the matter to the director for approval. You should hear back from me in a few days."

A few days. Would she be alive that long? Still, there was no alternative but to thank him, accept the file folder with the printed document and walk back out to the lobby to wait for Jesse. A quick glance at the parking lot showed he'd left, maybe to visit his mother or uncle. Or take Kip for a walk—it would be just like him to take care of her dog as well as she did.

She shot off a quick text to let him know she was done, then flipped to her father's letter naming the charity. What was this organization? Why had he never mentioned it? The whole thing felt a little fishy, and yet there was her father's signature at the bottom of the page. When she tapped the name into an internet search, a website came up, detailing the charity's involvement in educating and providing for underprivileged children.

The address was listed on the Contact page. A local charity, based right here in Jackson, as Mike had said. She tapped the number and street into her maps app, then tugged the end of her braid. He'd been right about the location— it was only a few blocks away. She could walk there and back in a matter of minutes.

After pulling up her text app, she sent the address to Jesse. Going to check it out. Be back here in fifteen minutes.

Following the map app was always a little disorienting on foot, but she figured out the right direction and strode quickly up the sidewalk.

Despite how rotten the day had been, the fresh air and exercise felt good. Almost invigorating, even. Was there a chance she'd rushed things, deciding to sell? Mike was going to contact Fitz, but that didn't mean the deal was sealed until she signed a contract. Maybe the police would get a lead in the next couple of days, and she'd find a way to keep both her sanity *and* the ranch.

Her route led her behind Jackson Financial and down a couple of blocks, then to the right. This section of town was older and not as nicely kept, but that made sense for a charity, didn't it? Rent was notoriously high in Jackson, and you wouldn't want the bulk of your fundraising to go toward the bills. But as she approached the address, she frowned at the tall brick building with its crumbling facade.

This place looked more than low rent; it looked aban- doned. A chill tracked across her arms, raising goose bumps on her skin. She glanced both ways up and down the street, but no one was in sight. It was still broad daylight, barely 4:00 p.m. No one was going to try anything. In fact, no one even knew she was here, except Jesse—though he hadn't responded to her text yet. She'd take a quick peek in the window, and maybe go inside if there was a secretary, just to get more information. Then she'd be back to Jackson Financial in a matter of minutes. Easy peasy.

She checked the street number she'd entered into Google Maps, scanning the shuttered glass doors of the buildings as she walked. In some places, the glass had been punched out and boarded over. For Rent signs hung in most of the windows.

Then her gaze fell on a black mailbox fixed to the brick wall near a door. The letters CUWW had been affixed to the box with peeling white stickers. She read the number above the door, then double-checked against her phone. This was the place.

Grime coated the inside of the glass door, making it impossible to see inside. She walked a few paces down the sidewalk to see inside the storefront. No lights inside. Glare from the setting sun reflected off the glass, so she cupped her hands around her face for a better view of the interior. Spiders walked through her stomach. There was nothing in there—just a few broken fixtures and pipes lying on the floor.

What was going on?

She needed to call Jesse, ASAP. But as she tapped into her contacts, movement in the nearby shadows of the next storefront sent a shock of adrenaline through her veins. She jerked her attention up from her phone, turning in the direction of the shifting shape.

Only to find a gun pointing directly at her, and behind it, the snarling face of Gordon Davis, the man who'd abducted her earlier.

"You're coming with me, Ms. Madsen."

"It's time to tell me the truth, Uncle Rob." Jesse hadn't even bothered taking a seat. With the way his uncle relaxed on the leather sofa, drinking glass in hand, Jesse's feet insisted on pacing back and forth. How could the man stay so cool after what had happened at Fitz's? Jesse had told him the entire tale as soon as his uncle had let him inside. "I know you and Sadie's father used to be friends. And then suddenly you weren't, and a few months later he didn't want anything to do with me, either. What happened?"

Rob's lips curled into a fake smile that made anger flare in Jesse's stomach. It was the same look his uncle gave clients while he worked a deal entirely in his favor. "Jesse, what difference does it make now? That's all water under the bridge. And my history with the Madsens won't help Sadie's situation."

Jesse flopped into a seat and cracked his knuckles. "She's going to sell to Fitz." Just saying it aloud made his stomach clench. It was like the final, inevitable conclusion to the train wreck he'd started so many years ago when he'd left her.

His uncle frowned, then set his glass on the coffee table. "I'm sorry to hear that. Dale would've been sorry, too." He sighed. "He was a good friend."

"Then tell me what happened." He leaned forward, pinning his uncle with a firm gaze. The man was slippery as an eel when he wanted to be, but Jesse wasn't going to relent this time.

Rob nodded. "I guess it won't hurt now. Maybe Sadie will even reconsider when she hears. About the time you two were in college and first started dating, Dale and I were out riding on his land when we came across a limestone deposit with a tiny bit of oil seeping up through a crack. You can imagine how excited we were at a discovery like that. Dale did a little research and found out the estate hadn't been split, so he still owned the mineral rights. I knew a guy who could evaluate the land to see if there would be enough worth drilling, so we had him come out to run some tests." His gaze fixed on Jesse. "He found more oil. Most likely a big well of it, not far from the house."

Jesse folded his arms over his chest, frowning. "That doesn't explain why you fought. Why didn't Dale say something? Or drill it himself?"

"That's why we fought." Rob picked at an invisible fleck on his suit jacket. "I saw you and Sadie were headed toward marriage, so I urged him to drill. The extra money would've been a real boost to you as you were starting out. But Dale refused. Insisted he wanted to keep the land intact, and he made me promise never to tell Sadie. After that, no matter what I did or said, he seemed to think I was pressuring him into drilling. He wouldn't let it go. The obsession grew to the point that he thought you were only after the oil."

Understanding flashed through Jesse's mind. *That* was why Dale had accused him of wanting the ranch more than his daughter. It wasn't actually about the Double M, it was the cache of black gold beneath the land, and neither Jesse nor Sadie had known anything about it.

"That's why he ran me off," he murmured, and Rob nodded.

"Yes. I tried to tell him you didn't know, but he didn't believe me. His paranoia had gotten out of control."

He grew silent for a moment, and Jesse glanced down at his phone to check the time. Two new texts had come from Sadie, one saying she was done with Mike and the other giving the address of the charity, which she was going to check out. Good, maybe she'd get a lead.

"Thanks," he said, standing up. "I appreciate your honesty."

"Of course." Uncle Rob shook his hand. "And please let me know if I can help Sadie in any way." He sounded sincere, but then Uncle Rob had a knack for saying exactly what the other person needed to hear. If Jesse had learned anything from living with him during his teenage years, it was that the man always worked things out to his benefit. The situation with Dale Madsen might've been the one time he'd failed to get what he wanted. No wonder he'd been reluctant to share.

On his way out the door, Jesse paused. "Do you know anything about Children's United Way of Wyoming?"

Rob slid his hands into his pockets, and his Adam's apple bobbed. "It sounds familiar. Is it local?"

"Never mind. Thanks." He'd better get over there to check on Sadie.

Kip barked and wedged his nose through the crack in the truck's window as Jesse walked up to the driver's side. "Good boy," he said, scratching the collie behind the ears. "We'll get you outside to run soon."

He punched the address into his maps app and drove the short route from his uncle's condo back into the denser part of town. The charity was close to Jackson Financial, but he didn't like the look of the street. If Jackson had a sketchy side, this was it. He parked in an empty spot, then helped Kip out of the truck.

"Come on, boy. Let's find Sadie." When he approached the building, he frowned. The place was empty and had clearly been so for a long time, judging by the piles of refuse and dirt inside. Where was Sadie? Had she walked back to Jackson Financial to wait for him?

Unease skittered through his system. He didn't like not knowing where she was, not with those men still on the loose.

Near his feet, Kip nosed the ground, sniffing his way up to the door and back. Then he whined, straining at the leash.

"Do you smell her? Good dog. Find Sadie!" Jesse gave him more slack, following close behind as Kip tugged ahead up the sidewalk. He nosed the ground, his tail wagging, then stopped and barked at a narrow alley separating two buildings. A knot twisted inside Jesse's chest. Had someone taken her back here?

"Quiet, Kip," he said. "Let's go." He jogged with the dog into the dark alley, dodging puddles leftover from the previous night's rain.

Kip led him around the back and into a small loading area. Jesse and the dog froze, scanning the area for any sign of Sadie. Or trouble.

Then a voice carried from behind a metal door that had been wedged open with a block of wood. His blood chilled at the words.

"Ms. Madsen, your time is up."

ELEVEN

Sadie knew that the appropriate response right now was fear, but all she could feel was anger—cold, icy fury building inside her veins. She had trusted Mike Schmidt. Her father had trusted him, too. And he'd set her up.

There was no other explanation. He'd told her the charity was close by, urged her to check it out. *And* he'd been distracted by something on his phone right after she'd read her father's letter.

Then a worm of doubt niggled at her insides. What if Mike hadn't ever followed up on the charity? Her father was the one who had chosen it. Why had her father chosen a nonexistent charity?

But *someone* had put the letters on the mailbox and created the website.

Her head threatened to explode. None of it made sense. And now this hired gun had tied her up in a chair and was threatening to kill her.

"Who hired you?" she belted out. His finger inched closer to the trigger, forcing a wave of panic through her. "Was it Mike? Mike Schmidt from Jackson Financial?"

Even as she said it, she knew it didn't make sense. At least, not the full picture. What would Mike stand to gain?

As cotrustee, would he have the authority to change the beneficiary in the event of her death? Or, since he only acted as a representative for the bank, could it be someone higher up in the chain? The manila folder he'd given her lay off to the side where she'd been forced to drop it, the pages sprawling across the dirty floor.

Davis laughed, a guttural sound that made goose bumps pop on her arms. "You're never going to know, are you, missy? Now shut up and let's get this over with."

Her breath stilled in her chest, and she closed her eyes, offering a silent prayer. After everything she'd done, it hadn't been enough to save the things that mattered in this life. But this life wasn't what was most important, was it? Peace flooded her heart at the thought of being with Jesus. *You take over, Lord. I've made a big enough mess. It's in Your hands now.*

A loud slamming sound split the quiet of the room, but no impact hit her head or chest. Then a dog barked, and her eyes flew open as Kip raced into the room and leaped at the man.

Davis swiveled with the gun.

"Kip!" Sadie screamed.

Before Davis could fire, Kip crashed into him, knocking him to the ground. The man shoved Kip off and rolled onto his knees, aiming for Jesse as he rushed in through the open door, gun in his hands.

Her heart stopped as Davis fired his weapon. Jesse ducked as the shot went wide. He raised his own gun and pulled the trigger. There was another sharp crack, and then Davis fell backward clutching his shoulder. In a second Jesse was on him, removing his gun and cuffing his hands behind his back.

Keeping Davis pinned, he looked at Sadie. The tender, fierce expression in his eyes threatened to melt the safety walls she'd built around her heart. "Did he hurt you?"

"No, I'm all right. Other than being abducted *again*."

Kip ran up to her, nuzzling her legs and the hands tied behind her back with his warm, wet nose. "Good boy," she said, relief crashing through her system. *Thank You, Lord, for protecting Jesse and my dog.* And He'd saved her, too. Maybe she still had more to accomplish on this earth before she went home to heaven.

"Let me call this one in." Jesse flashed his phone at her, then called the police and made the report. Beneath his knee, the man moaned. "Don't try anything, and you'll live. Kip, watch him."

Her dog barked as if agreeing to guard duty, then sat near the man. Jesse stood and, using a pocketknife, cut the ropes binding Sadie to the old metal chair Davis had tied her to. He helped her up, and almost of their own accord, her arms slipped around his back. She pressed her face into his soft shirt.

"Hey, it's okay." He laid a hand on her hair and the other on her back, holding her close. For a moment, all the horrors of the past few days vanished into a delicious feeling of safety and comfort in his arms.

Then Jesse's phone rang, and they sprang apart. "It's Rob," he said, glancing at the number, then answering.

She frowned. What could Rob Clark want?

"Jesse here… Okay. She was just attacked again… At the charity, which doesn't exist. I caught the guy, though. We don't know who—" He broke off, listening for a minute. "That's fine. I'll text after we wrap up here." He ended the call, then turned to her. "He says he did some digging on Fitz. Apparently, he found something he wants to discuss with us right away."

She massaged her temples. Would this day, this week, never end? "Can he just bring it to the cops?"

"He wants to run it by us first. He's at one of his nearby rental properties doing an evaluation for repairs, so I said we'd stop by after we wrap up here." Something shifted in his gaze, and a muscle worked in his jaw. "I need to fill you in on what I learned about him and your father."

"Did you get more details about why they fought?" She'd never wanted to confront her father, but she had asked her mom more than once. Cathy would only say that they'd argued over a business deal that hadn't worked out.

"Yeah, Rob finally told me. But first—" He cut off as sirens blared outside the back door.

A pair of Jackson city police officers entered, followed by Deputy Freeman. While the officers tended to the man who was down, Freeman approached Jesse and Sadie. "Sounds like you two have been busy."

"You could say that." Jesse turned to Sadie. "What happened? The charity is obviously long gone."

"If it ever existed in the first place," she said grimly, stooping to pick up her spilled file folder. Over the next few minutes, she detailed exactly what had happened, including Mike Schmidt's suggestion she walk over to check the place out. "There's still a website for CUWW. My guess is that it's a fake, and somebody from Jackson Financial set it up with the plan to name a new beneficiary after they had me killed."

Freeman tapped his pen against his notepad. "We'll need to look into the legalities of a situation like that. This might be enough to issue a search warrant for Jackson Financial's records, but I'll need to talk to the judge."

"Is there a public record of who created the charity?" Jesse asked. "Or do we think it's not even a legal entity?"

"I assumed it would have to be a legally recognized charity for my father to name it as beneficiary, or for Jackson Financial to approve it, but who knows." Sadie dragged a hand down her braid.

"We'll find out who owns the domain name for the website," Freeman said, jotting notes. When he finished, he glanced between them. "I'll let you know what we learn. And as soon as the state assigns a lawyer to Justin Barts and his sidekick over there, we'll see what we can learn from them." As he spoke, the two officers escorted Davis outside.

"Any leads on the third one, Mitchell Warden?" Jesse asked. He turned to Sadie. "You didn't see him, right?"

She shook her head. "Just Davis."

"If he was in the area, he probably cleared out when he heard the sirens," Freeman said. "Deputy Griggs is monitoring the reports on missing and stolen vehicles in case that gives us a lead. You know where to find me if anything else comes up."

They shook hands with him, then went outside. The sun was slinking behind the mountains in the west, deepening the shadows behind the building and lending a hint of evening coolness to the air. Sadie wrapped her arms across her chest as Kip trotted next to her.

"The truck's out front," Jesse said. "I'll let my uncle know we're on the way."

"What did he say about my father?" she asked as they turned into the alley and walked toward the street.

"He knew about the oil." He glanced at her. "Did you know he'd hired a geologist before you did?"

He had? She frowned. "No, neither he nor Mom ever said anything. I must've been away at school when they had someone come out."

"Apparently my uncle was with him when they first discovered it. Rob pushed for your father to drill, but Dale didn't want to. He insisted on keeping it secret. My uncle says he grew more and more paranoid, until eventually he stopped trusting either Rob or…" He let the words trail off. "I'm sorry. I just want you to know how much I respected your father. He was a good man, regardless of what happened with Uncle Rob."

Wait a second… Was Jesse afraid of hurting her feelings by saying negative things about her father? And what had he been about to say?

Like gears clicking into place, suddenly everything made sense. "Or you."

"What?" As they spilled out onto the street, he paused, tilting his head to one side.

There was his truck, just down the way past the fake charity. "Come on," she said, taking his arm and pulling him toward it. "My dad stopped trusting your uncle Rob *and* you. That's what you were going to say."

"Well, yeah, but how did you—"

"He told me I was better off without you." The words had stung worse than the bite of a whip when her father had first spoken them to her. She hadn't believed him then, and now—now she understood. "Right after you left. He said you were going to leave eventually, so it was better you did it then than string me along."

Jesse dragged a hand over his face, then pulled his keys

out of his pocket and opened the door for her. "And all I did was prove him right, didn't I?"

The words came out etched in bitterness and regret so potent it made her heart ache. She reached for him, more to offer comfort than anything else, but he'd already turned away to help Kip into the back seat.

After he walked around and climbed into the driver seat, she laid a hand on his arm. "What did he say to you?" When he dropped his eyes, avoiding her gaze, she squeezed his arm gently. "Jesse, I *knew* you. If one of us was wrong about you, me or my father, it wasn't me. You weren't the kind of man who'd leave unless you had an incredibly good reason. What did he say to you?"

Now they'd come to the point. Jesse hadn't intended to ever let the conversation get this far, and yet here he was, pouring out all the bitter details of his breach with her father. But how could he not answer? So much had been kept from her all these years as she fended for herself. She probably felt the same way he had with Uncle Rob, like all he wanted was for someone to be honest, no matter how painful it was.

That didn't make it any easier forcing the ugly words out. "He said a lot of things, but pretty much the same thing. He said, 'Jesse Taylor, you're not good enough for her. She needs someone who'll love her for who she is, not for her land. You're going to break her heart, and I will *never* give my blessing to you.' He could still hear—*feel*—the bitter resentment in Dale's tone, stinging worse than a snakebite since he'd respected Dale so much."

"Oh, Jesse…" Her fingers dug lightly into his arm, where her hand rested warm on his shirtsleeve.

"And the worst part is…" He swallowed down the thick lump in his throat. "I believed him. I was only twenty-two, just out of college with only the barest idea of what the future would look like, other than being with you." A smile pulled at his lips. That was all he'd wanted back then, the only thing that had mattered. "Even though his accusations weren't fair, I didn't know how to stand up to him. He was Dale Madsen. Your *father*. And if he said I wasn't good enough for you…" He shook his head. "I was terrified of letting you down, especially since Uncle Rob had already convinced me I was a disappointment. So I proved them both right and walked away. It was the worst decision of my life, and I'll never forgive myself for how much I hurt you."

When he finally dared to look at her, her eyes had gone glossy.

She blinked a few times, squeezing his arm again. "Thank you for telling me what happened. I never understood how I'd misjudged you so badly. I *knew* you weren't a coward who'd get scared of commitment and run." She pulled her hand back, then folded it with the other one in her lap. "My father *was* a good man, but he wasn't perfect. I'm sorry he treated you that way, Jesse. Your uncle, too. He had no business tearing you down like that. You've always been amazing. And—" she bit her lip "—I forgive you. It did hurt, terribly, but I understand now why you did what you did."

She spoke the words slowly, and it took a few moments for him to fully grasp what she'd said, the olive branch she'd just held out. His throat felt sticky and thick at the peace offering he didn't deserve. But God had forgiven him, too, hadn't He? Jesse thought of the Bible verse he'd memorized so long ago: *If we confess our sins, He is faith-*

*ful and just to forgive us our sins, and to cleanse us from
all unrighteousness.*

"Thank you," he finally squeezed out. "I… That means
a lot to me."

She nodded, and her throat bobbed as she blinked again.
Something had shifted in the space between them, as if the
air had been cleared of some lingering toxic residue. The
gold flecks in her brown eyes shone in a way he hadn't
seen in years. He could feel the same lightness buoying
up inside his chest.

Then she glanced away, and heat stole across the back
of his neck as he realized he'd been staring into her eyes.

Right, they had things to do. And her forgiveness didn't
mean they'd be rekindling their old relationship. He *hoped*
they could be friends now, but realistically they'd be moving in separate circles once this was all over. The last thing
he wanted to do was hurt her again.

He cleared his throat, then twisted the key in the ignition. "We'd better get going. Uncle Rob is waiting for us.
He's got some dinner meeting he has to get to."

"Yes," she said firmly. "What's the address? I can navigate."

After she'd typed it in, he followed her directions to a
stretch of warehouses on the fringe of town.

"Is that it?" He pointed to a big blue building up ahead
that bore the fading outline of a sign that had long since
been removed.

"It must be." Sadie glanced at the map on her phone.

Jesse turned the truck into the nearly empty lot and
pulled into a spot near the front entrance next to a sleek
black Lexus. One of the warehouse doors had been propped
open with a broken piece of cinder block.

"Your uncle is a busy man," Sadie said, surveying the faded exterior of the building. "How many jobs does he have?"

"He's always been this way." Jesse shut off the engine. "Always making the most of his connections and looking for a new way to make a buck. The only reason he's stuck with real estate so long is because that's where the cash is in this city. Everyone wants a place in Jackson."

They climbed out of the truck.

Sadie paused with her hand on the door. "Think it's okay to bring Kip?"

"I don't see why not. Nobody's using the place." He opened the rear door. Kip bounded over, wagging his tail and nuzzling Jesse's hands. Laughing, he helped the dog down. "Yes, you can come, boy."

Together they walked up to the front, and Jesse pulled the metal door open enough to let them inside, then let it fall back against the cinder block. Overhead, round fluorescent lights flickered high in the ceiling, illuminating a vast, empty concrete floor. Water dripped somewhere in the distance.

"Uncle Rob?" Jesse's voice echoed in the huge, empty space. He glanced at Sadie. "Maybe he's in the back. I should've texted to tell him we were on the way."

"It took us a while with the police." She glanced back at Kip, who was sniffing the area near the door. "Come on, Kip."

His uncle had said he was here to evaluate the repairs— maybe that dripping water was a clue to where he'd gone. They took a few steps inside, their boots clicking on the concrete. More lights were on in the back, shining through

an open door that probably led into a smaller office or storage area.

"Uncle Rob?" he called again. Sadie glanced at him, her
eyebrows raised, and he lifted his hands. "He said he'd be
here. And his car is out front. At least, I'm assuming it's his
car." Who else driving a Lexus would be hanging around
an empty warehouse?

A loud *thunk* sounded behind them. Jesse spun on his
heel in time to see the front door fall shut behind two men
who had just entered.

His uncle, and someone whose back was turned. A repairman? He caught Sadie's eye. The crease between her
eyes matched his own frown. Rob hadn't mentioned anyone else being here.

"Hey, Uncle Rob," he called. They walked back toward
the door, stopping a few feet away.

"Jesse. Sadie." Rob nodded their way, his expression
grim. Whatever news he had to share didn't look good.

But what was the other man doing to the door? It almost
looked as if—

The door latch clicked as it locked into place. Then the
man turned, and Jesse caught a full view of his face beneath
the overhead light. Next to him, Sadie gasped.

Mitchell Warden—the missing third man who'd been
chasing them this whole time. And he was holding a gun.

TWELVE

Jesse froze. On instinct he threw an arm out in front of Sadie, as if that would make any difference should the man decide to shoot.

"Uncle Rob?" He turned to his uncle, trying to make the pieces fit together in any way that made sense. "Tell me you don't have anything to do with this."

"Sorry, Jesse. I can't do that." His uncle raised one hand in a gesture of helplessness, then pulled out a handgun of his own from a holster concealed beneath his suit jacket. "Looks like you made the wrong choice again, I'm afraid. This is the end of the line for you and Sadie."

Kip, who'd been trotting around the big empty space with his tongue lolling to one side, seemed to sense the trouble and came running toward Sadie. When Warden stiffened, Sadie held a hand out at her side.

"Kip, sit," she commanded. The dog dropped down next to her, his head up and eyes alert. "Stay."

"I'm sure you're armed, Jesse," Rob drawled. "Slide the gun over to me and put your hands up. You, too, Sadie." He waved the gun her direction, making Jesse flinch.

One wrong move, and he'd never get to hear Sadie's voice again. But years of law enforcement had drilled into him to never give up his weapon. That gun could mean the difference between life and death.

So instead of going for his holster, he raised both hands over his head, hoping his uncle wouldn't overreact. Maybe there was still a chance to talk him off this ledge.

"Uncle Rob, what's going on?" he asked, fighting to keep his voice calm and soothing. "We're just here to talk, like you asked."

"It's too late now. We both know how this scene ends." A look of sympathy crossed Rob's face. "This will be very hard on your mother, but I promise I'll take care of her the way I always have. For the record, I never wanted you to get involved at all. If you'd just let me handle things with Sadie without interfering, we wouldn't be here."

"*Handle* things with me?" Sadie scowled, but her hands trembled as she held them up near her head. "So you're the one who hired those men to come after me? Did you cause all the other accidents at the Double M, too?"

Rob shrugged. "How else was I supposed to get you to sell? Dale never would. Then when you learned about the oil, I figured you'd never let the ranch go, so the only option was to get rid of you." His lips curled. "Permanently."

"But how would killing Sadie help you?" Jesse frowned.

"The charity…" she breathed, her gaze darting to his. And then suddenly it all made sense.

Jesse clenched his jaw. "*You* set up the fake charity," he said through gritted teeth. "Of course, that's something you would do." And know *how* to do. His uncle's influence stretched like tentacles through this town. "Did you convince that advisor at Jackson Financial to play along? He'd have to know that charity wasn't legit."

"And he set me up," Sadie muttered.

"Unfortunately, you didn't leave us much choice." Rob waved the gun between them as he talked. "Since you wouldn't just believe the letter we faked. If my special nephew hadn't intervened, that could've been the end of the story. Mike wasn't excited about the scheme, but it's amazing what some people will do for money."

"Hold up. You faked the letter?" she asked. "So my dad never designated your charity as beneficiary?"

"No, he wanted to choose a real charity, of all things." Rob laughed. "What good would that have done me? So as soon as Mike was on board with the plan, he made a few simple alterations to your father's actual letter and inserted my charity instead. Dale never knew." He tilted his head to one side as he glanced between them. "Of course, all this would've been spoiled if you two had actually gotten married and had little brats. Good thing Dale at least listened to me about my conniving nephew."

Anger had been slowly building in Jesse's gut as his uncle talked, and now it threatened to boil over like an erupting volcano. All those years absorbing his uncle's negative messages, and now he finally knew exactly what kind of man Rob was. He balled his hands into fists above his head, inhaling slowly through his nose and exhaling through his mouth before he did something rash.

"What did you tell my father about Jesse?" Sadie's voice came out in a low, shaking growl.

"Look at you two, getting so upset. I hope you know it wasn't anything personal, Sadie. I always liked you. You've got spunk. But obviously I couldn't let you marry Jesse. Dale and I had already fallen out, so it wasn't hard to hint that Jesse agreed with me about drilling. I didn't even have

to suggest that Jesse was only marrying you for the oil—
Dale reached that conclusion on his own."

"I didn't even know about the oil," Jesse snapped. "But
if she hadn't married me, she could just as easily have married someone else! And then you'd still get no ranch." He
glanced at her as he rattled off the angry words, but there
it was—the truth—written plain as day in the heartbroken
expression on her face.

"I couldn't marry anyone else," she whispered, her eyes
glossy.

"See?" His uncle smirked. "Poor lovesick babies."

His heart twisted in his chest. Had Sadie loved him all
this time? And what about him? He'd never stopped loving *her*, had he? When he dug deep, beneath his shame and
regret and Dale's harsh words, the well of aching sorrow
that had filled him for so long after he'd left her was still
there. Covered, maybe, but not diminished.

In fact, it hurt far worse now than it had only a week
ago before he'd seen her again. Every minute with her only
reminded him of what he'd lost.

What he might lose permanently if they didn't get out
of this situation alive.

His uncle waved a hand. "Not that it mattered. Even
if Sadie *had* gotten over you and found some other man,
he'd be the one here right now instead of you." His words
hit Jesse like a punch to the gut, making his knees wobble.

Another man could've married Sadie. Another man
could be the one protecting her and caring for her. Holding her close. Sharing her future—or what was left of it.

And he'd let her go all because of his uncle's greed and
Dale Madsen's unfounded concerns and his own fear of not
being enough. If they lived through this, he was going to

tell Sadie exactly how he felt. Even if it meant risking her saying no if she wasn't ready to trust him again. He could live with her decision—he just couldn't live with his own.

"It's unfortunate we had to end up here," Rob said, "but it's time to quit dragging things out. Once Sadie is gone, the estate will revert to the charity. Which, I might add, is a legal entity even if it's not currently engaged in any charitable activities. Maybe one day."

Yeah, right.

"What about Stanley Fitz?" Jesse asked. If he could keep Rob talking a little longer, maybe he could figure out a way to get them out of here alive. They hadn't told anyone where they were going, but he still had his gun. If there was a way to create a distraction...

"What about him?" Rob said carelessly.

"Is he involved in this?" Sadie shifted her weight from one foot to the other. Her hands had started to sag from the strain of holding them over her head for so long.

Rob waved the gun at her. "Get those hands back up, Sadie. No, Fitz just made a convenient scapegoat. He's wanted the ranch for years. Used to make offers to your parents, too."

"You sent the men after us when we visited his ranch," Sadie said. Yet another piece of the puzzle that suddenly made sense. His uncle was the one who'd urged them to visit Fitz's ranch. That explained how his hired thugs had known where to find them. With property that huge, it wouldn't have been hard for them to find a back way across the fields to his house.

"If Davis and Warden had only succeeded in killing her then, you could've lived, Jesse." Rob shrugged apologetically.

"But receiving my trust won't do you any good in jail," Sadie said. "The police have already caught two of your minions." She turned a glare on the third man. "It'll be your turn next. If you think those two won't take a deal and talk, you've got another think coming."

The man kept his gun on Jesse, and if her words had any effect on him, it didn't show on his face.

"I'm not a total amateur, you know." Rob's lips curled. "You'd be surprised at what one can accomplish with the right leverage. But you don't need to worry about me, I won't be going to jail. How can I be held responsible for your lovers' quarrel and murder-suicide? It's a shame I stumbled upon it and had to witness the messy aftermath." His face contorted into a fake grimace. "And now…"

The gun, which Rob had been holding almost carelessly, straightened as he extended his arm and leveled it at Sadie. He stepped toward her, staying out of reach but close enough there was no way he'd miss.

Fear shot through Jesse's system until he could taste it, dry and bitter on his tongue. Like mistakes and regret and broken chances. His hand slipped lower, poised to reach for the gun at his waist.

Near Sadie's feet, Kip growled.

His uncle's finger rested on the trigger as he sighted down the barrel. "Goodbye, Sadie."

Everything went suddenly cold, as if Sadie could already feel death sweeping over her mortal body. *Thank You, Jesus, that I'll be with You.* She wished she could've talked to Jesse one more time. Told him how much he'd always meant to her. And still did.

Then Kip, her obedient, beautiful collie, broke her stay

command and lunged across the concrete floor, his lips pulled back and teeth bared.

The gun went off with a biting crack as Kip clamped his teeth into Rob's leg. There was a sharp *ping* somewhere behind Sadie as the bullet hit metal.

She screamed, diving for Kip, terrified Rob would kill her dog. More shots fired as she grabbed Kip around the middle, pulling the collie away from Rob.

Warden fell to the ground next to the door, clutching his stomach. His gun skittered across the floor.

Fire blazed in Rob's eyes as his face contorted into a hideous mask of anger. He swiveled the gun down, its barrel mere feet away from where Sadie held Kip back. A shot fired now would kill both her and Kip.

She squeezed the dog close, pinning Rob with a glare. If he wanted to kill her in cold blood, she wasn't going to close her eyes and make it easy for him.

"No!" Jesse yelled, his voice cracking.

Another gunshot split the air, echoing off the metal walls and concrete floor of the big space.

Kip barked, and Sadie clutched him tight, expecting a shock of pain any second now.

But instead, Rob collapsed to the floor. The gun flew from his hand, going off when it hit the ground. The bullet ricocheted harmlessly, tearing out a chunk of concrete. Rob rolled over, straining for the weapon, but Jesse reached it first. Keeping his weapon trained on Rob, he crossed the distance to collect Warden's gun.

"Don't move," Jesse ordered. He glanced between the two fallen men. "Either of you. Sadie," he said without taking his eyes off the men, "can you call the police? We'll need an ambulance."

She pressed her face into Kip's fur, breathing a deep, shuddering breath of his warm doggy scent, then released him. After tapping through to an emergency dispatcher, she opted to stay on the line as they waited for the police to arrive just in case Rob Clark tried anything.

But he only sat in tense silence, a scowl crumpling his forehead, as he pressed a hand to a dark, wet patch spreading across his leg.

Jesse had had to shoot him. His own uncle. She bit her lip, glancing between him and Rob, but Jesse kept his focus entirely on the two villains.

Within minutes, sirens sounded outside, and gravel crunched as squad cars pulled into the lot.

Sadie pushed herself onto shaky legs and walked around behind Jesse to the door, giving Warden a wide berth. When she reached the door, she flipped the latch to release the lock, then pushed it open.

Two Jackson PD officers climbed out of a squad car, followed a moment later by Deputies Freeman and Griggs from the Sheriff's Department. When Sadie saw their familiar faces, something cracked inside, and heat built in her sinuses, making her eyes sting. Could it be possible this was really over?

She managed to keep herself together as she held the door open for them, and they passed inside. Another siren sounded close by, and an ambulance turned onto the street, its lights gleaming red against the darkening evening shadows. She propped the door open again with the cinder block and went back inside.

Jesse was handing the two weapons over to Deputy Griggs, who placed them inside evidence bags. The Jackson officers crouched near the fallen men, cuffing them both and applying pressure to their wounds.

Kip ran over to her, his tongue lolling out one side again, breath coming in little pants. Seeing him whole and intact made the fire in her sinuses flare, and she blinked rapidly.

"The ambulance is almost here," she announced.

Jesse glanced away from Deputy Griggs, his eyes locking on hers. The swirl of emotion in his blue gaze made her heart stutter. For a second, she wished everyone else would vanish and it could be just the two of them, alone.

Abruptly he walked away from the deputy and came striding toward her, like some invisible cord that linked them together had snapped taut. Then he was in front of her, studying her face with an intensity that obliterated her last-ditch effort to stay strong. Tears pooled in her eyes and her throat burned.

His arms swept around her, pressing her close in his strong embrace, and her senses filled with the soft aroma of leather and cedarwood. She nuzzled her cheek against the soft cotton of his shirt, drinking in the comfort and safety and strength he offered.

"It's over," he whispered into her hair. "You're safe, Sadie. And I'm so, so sorry for everything."

It took a moment for his words to filter through the haze in her brain. Why was he apologizing? As if any of this was his fault?

She pushed against his chest, then wiped her cheeks as she looked up at him. He loosened his grasp, his arms falling slowly to his sides, leaving her cold all over. Did he think she was pushing him away? That she didn't want him, despite everything they'd been through together?

"Jesse." She said his name softly, shaking her head.

"Rob's choices aren't your fault. He set us all on this course years ago, long before you had even proposed to me."

"But if you and I hadn't started dat—"

She pressed a finger to his lips. "If we hadn't dated, he still would've come after the Double M because of the oil and his friendship with my father. And I would've missed out on some of the happiest years of my life."

He closed his eyes, tucking his chin. When he reopened them, the blue depths were pools of liquid emotion. "Sadie... I should've talked to you first. When your father accused me of wanting the ranch and not wanting you. When he said I wasn't good enough. I felt so much fear and shame, but what's bothered me even more all these years is the way I left without giving you a voice in the decision. I let him decide for me, and then I let him decide for you." A muscle twitched in his cheek, and when he spoke again, his voice was thick. "I treated you with disrespect, Sadie, and I'm so sorry."

His words cut deep and sharp like a scalpel straight to the scarred part of her heart she'd tried to ignore for so long. Because that was the part that had always bothered her the most—that Jesse had made his choice without even giving her a chance. He'd never heard her side of the story, or what she wanted, because he never gave her the chance to tell him. And what she'd wanted had been him, no matter what her father had had to say about it.

If she were being honest, what she *still* wanted was him. Because while she appreciated his apology, it didn't make a dent in the vast heap of longing that had built up in her heart over the past seven years.

Somewhere behind her, she could sense the motion of the EMTs as they carried the two injured men out on stretchers.

The deputies would have questions for her and Jesse; they'd need to do an entire debrief. But at this moment there was only one thing she wanted in the world, and he was standing right in front of her.

"Do I get a voice now?" she asked softly. "Will you listen to what I have to say?"

Jesse lifted his chin, then nodded slowly as if he were still afraid. And yet light glinted in his eyes, reflecting off his blue irises like sunlight off a glacial moraine lake.

"The hardest part about you leaving wasn't how much it hurt then. It was how much it's hurt every single day since. I've never stopped loving you." At her soft words, his lips turned up at the corners into a gentle, hopeful smile. "I tried to forget about you. I tried to keep busy with the ranch and the horses and all my projects, but being with you again has only made the truth obvious. I'm hopelessly in love with you, Jesse Taylor."

"You are?" A crease formed between his brows. "Even after all the ways I've let you down?"

"What ways?" she scoffed. "Other than the day you left, you've never let me down. In fact, I wouldn't be alive and kicking right now if it weren't for you. Nobody knows how to make me feel safe or handle my stubborn streak—" her lips cracked into a grin "—the way you do."

Kip chose that moment to wedge between them, cramming his muscular, furry body between their legs.

Jesse laughed, and Sadie nodded down at the collie. "See? Even my dog loves you."

His expression sobered, and he placed a hand on her cheek, running his thumb gently along her chin. "Sadie, I—" his Adam's apple bobbed "—I've already told you that walking away from you was the worst mistake I ever made.

I never stopped loving you, either, not for a moment. You've always been part of my life, even when you didn't know it, because I couldn't forget you. I'd like nothing better than a second chance to prove to you that I'm a man of my word."

Warmth flooded her chest as she leaned into his touch. "You don't have to prove anything to me. I already know you're a man of your word."

"Will you—"

"Yes," she breathed.

He laughed, unshed tears glistening in his eyes. "You didn't hear the question."

"I couldn't wait that long to answer."

"Marry me?"

She nodded, blinking away the moisture in her eyes.

"I don't deserve you," he whispered. He leaned closer, and she stretched up until their lips met in a soft kiss filled with years of longing. Behind them, somebody clapped. They pulled apart, grinning at each other like two teenagers.

"You're stuck with me forever now," she said.

His tender gaze filled her with warmth from head to toe. "I can't imagine anything better."

EPILOGUE

Six months later

Sadie stood in front of the full-length mirror in her bedroom, watching as Jesse's mom, Lisa, finished tucking tiny sprigs of holly into her crown of braids. With her satin wedding gown and white veil, the effect was stunning.

"You look like a princess," Katrina said as Lisa stepped back. Sadie's best friend stood next to her in her crimson bridesmaid dress, and the two of them smiled at each other in the mirror. "I hope Jesse Taylor knows how blessed he is."

"He does." Sadie hugged her friend, then turned toward the door as Lottie and Zeke peeked in.

"Are you ready?" Zeke asked. He looked dashing in his tux.

She nodded, then hefted her skirts and followed the Nelsons through the house. A flood of emotions swirled beneath her ribs—happiness, nostalgia, sorrow that her parents weren't here. If her father hadn't been deceived by Rob, he would've been overjoyed to have such a son-in-law. She felt that truth deep in her bones.

"It's cold outside," Lottie warned when they reached the front door.

"What else can we expect at a Christmas wedding in Wyoming?" She laughed.

Freshly falling snow dusted her head and shoulders as they walked from the house to the pole barn. Ground had been broken on the new horse stables and the addition to the house that would hold the main guest wing, but the cold had set in before either was finished.

Jesse had offered to help find another place for the wedding and reception, but Sadie couldn't imagine getting married anywhere else.

And when it came down to it, the pole barn was the perfect spot. With the money they'd received from Rob for damages, she'd been able to not only settle the ranch's financial accounts but move forward with renovations. Jesse fully supported her dream of creating a beautiful space for guests. He intended to keep working at the national park until they were ready to open. After that, he had all sorts of plans to help their guests fully experience the natural beauty of the Tetons.

Zeke opened the door, revealing a small antechamber created by a set of screens. Thousands of tiny twinkling white lights dangled from the rafters above her. When they stepped inside, a hush fell over the assembled guests on the other side of the screens. A snort sounded below, and Sadie chuckled as she watched a dark shape move between the floorboards. The horses would be guests at the wedding, too.

And what more fitting place to seal their future than here, where they'd been split apart so many years before?

Yet the Lord, in His great mercy, had seen to it that they'd find their way back together.

A moment later the sweet strains of a guitar filled the barn with a wedding march. Sadie looped her arm through Zeke's, and he smiled at her. "Your father would've been so proud of you."

"Thank you," she said.

Lottie and Lisa rolled the screens back, and the small gathering of guests rose as the two women walked down the aisle, followed by Katrina in front of Sadie and Zeke. Kip trotted along beside her friend, carrying the wedding rings in a pouch tied to his collar. Time felt like it stood still as Sadie took in the twinkling lights and evergreen boughs decorating the barn. Then her gaze went to the end of the aisle, where Jesse stood waiting for her, and her breath lodged in her chest.

He looked exactly the way she'd always imagined he would, broad shoulders and narrow waist perfectly suited for a tuxedo. With his strong jawline and dark hair, on this day he resembled a Hollywood star more than a park ranger she'd loved all her adult life.

But it was the emotion shining in his eyes that made her float down the aisle on Zeke's arm. And when Zeke handed her to Jesse and she slid her hands into his, she finally felt at home. Together they made their promises before the Lord and their family and friends, then sealed their vows with a kiss.

"I love you," Jesse whispered as they pulled apart.

"I love you back." She smiled.

Then, despite Katrina's best attempts to hold him back, Kip wedged himself between Sadie's dress and Jesse's legs, leaving long crimped dog hairs all over his black pants. "Kip loves you, too."

They both laughed, celebrating God's goodness and the joyous beginning of their life together.

* * * * *

*If you enjoyed this story,
don't miss other exciting reads
by Kellie VanHorn!*

Discover more at LoveInspired.com

Dear Reader,

Thank you so much for going on this Wyoming adventure with Sadie, Jesse and me! The wild and majestic Teton mountain range is one of my favorite places to visit. My family loves camping in the national park, hiking the trails, swimming in the lakes and eating picnics where it's so beautiful we feel like we're in a postcard. Nearby Jackson is such a fun place, too, with its Western ambience, frequent summer rodeos and chuckwagon suppers. While I've taken a few liberties with the real-life setting to better serve the story, I hope you've come away with a small glimpse of how much I love this rugged and remote part of the country.

Jesse and Sadie have a lot to untangle in this story, don't they? Family secrets, their messy past relationship and new dangers. Like most of us, they'd rather sweep all of that under the rug, pretend it didn't happen and move on with their lives. But thankfully, the Lord doesn't let us wallow in muck; instead, He puts obstacles in our way to force us to deal with the things we'd rather avoid. Because of His great love for us, He gently offers us comfort and healing as He teaches us to be more like Christ. How grateful I am that one day we'll be made whole and complete and find our happy ending with Him!

I love hearing from readers, so please feel free to get in touch. You can find me on my Facebook page (Kellie VanHorn, Author) or subscribe to my newsletter at www.kellievanhorn.com.

Warm regards,
Kellie VanHorn

HARLEQUIN
Reader Service

Enjoyed your book?

Try the perfect subscription for Romance readers and get more great books like this delivered right to your door.

See why over 10+ million readers have tried Harlequin Reader Service.

Start with a Free Welcome Collection with free books and a gift—valued over $20.

Choose any series in print or ebook.
See website for details and order today:

   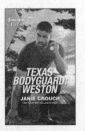

TryReaderService.com/subscriptions